The
Appearance of Things

This book is a work of fiction. Names, characters, places, and events either are products of the author's imagination or are used fictitiously. Any resemblance to actual events or locals or persons, living or dead, is entirely coincidental.

Copyright 2007 by Keith Swift

ISBN 978-0-6151-4442-9

"All men are deceived by the appearances of things, even Homer himself, who was the wisest man in Greece; for he was deceived by boys catching lice: they said to him, "What we have caught and what we have killed we have left behind, but what has escaped we bring with us."

Heraclitus

CHAPTER ONE

In the mid-seventeen-hundreds, a band of Spanish conquistadors followed a passage through the Santa Monica coastal mountain range and found itself in a natural basin that is now called the San Fernando Valley, where a river lined by reeds wound through waist-high grasslands and nourished a variety of fruits, nuts, and berries. There, in the shade of oak trees, they came across several small villages where they were welcomed by natives with food and drink.

The valley is now divided into small cities, and there is little left of the natural habitat but the surrounding mountain ranges and a lowland bird sanctuary to tell what it might have once looked like. The ancient river, in which steelhead trout returned to spawn, is the gray scar of a concrete drainage channel that washes plastic cups, aluminum cans, and other shards of urban civilization to the Pacific Ocean on which stout Cortez once gazed upon in wonder.

In the years that followed the militant Spaniards the valley has suffered territorial wars, local skirmishes, ground-water and air pollution, earthquakes, and even the partial melt-down of a secret nuclear reactor hidden deep in a laboratory in the Santa Susanna Mountains, which released a cloud of cancer-causing gas that drifted eastward over the land. Yet the valley has endured, and on sweltering summer days when thermal inversions prevent dust and other pollutants from escaping it smolders like a witch's caldron; a reminder perhaps of what is gone and what is yet to come. But on a winter morning, when the air is fresh and clean and the sun rises lemon-yellow through a lowland mist and the first songbirds stir in their nests among the reeds, it seems like a land of milk and honey, a land that was inhabited by indigenous Indians two thousand years before the Spaniards arrived, and which has since become the home to endless generations of immigrants.

In a park adjacent to the bird sanctuary a group of men are gathered on a field, preparing for a friendly game of soccer. Their breath is visible in the crisp morning air as they run in place or jog back and forth, warming their muscles. One group seems almost professional, as they trot out onto the field in matching uniforms, while the other seems to be in disarray and comprised of rank amateurs in unmatched uniforms. Their members are variously out of shape or overweight, and representative of the general working class. Among them is Joe, a Scotch immigrant electrician, Devin, an English immigrant waiter, Cruz, an illegal immigrant waiter, and three Americans, Shawn, a general contractor, Marty, a pudgy computer salesman, and Danny, a garrulous and overweight plumber. As one team warms up, with precision passes, the others can be heard bickering.

"Hey, Joe," Danny shouts, "where the hell is everybody?"

"I haven't a clue, mate," Joe replies.

"Marty, have you seen Steve?" Danny continues.

"No, he's probably in bed with something warm, which is where I should be," Marty grins.

Danny shakes his head in mock-disgust, and continues to shout.

"Shawn, have you seen Steve?"

"No, I haven't, but he hurt his ankle last week, so maybe he's decided not to play anymore."

"No, he's probably just running late," Joe observes, as Danny continues to shout.

"Well, what about the others?"

"I ran into Malcolm," Marty chimes in, "and he's not coming. He's working overtime; said he wants to put some dough away for Christmas."

"Jesus Christ!" Danny exclaims, melodramatically throwing down his towel and stamping on it. "Every stinking week it's something, isn't it? No wonder we never win. We're not a friggin team, and now we don't even have a goalie. Ah, shit, we might as well go home."

"How about we stop by the pub?" Marty grins. "That new Welsh waitress might be working, and I've got a feeling she can't wait to see me again."

"Don't be daft, Marty, she's just a kid," Joe smiles.

"Well, she's old enough to serve beer isn't she? And what am I, an old man?"

"You're a dirty old man, that's what you are," Joe chuckles.

"No I'm not," Marty grins, "I just appreciate feminine pulchritude."

"Where do you come off using filth like that?" Danny taunts.

"It's not filth. It's just fancy talk. It means, 'feminine beauty,' doesn't it, Dev?"

"Yeah, something like that," Devin agrees.

"Besides," Danny continues, "she's probably a nice Catholic girl."

"That's alright," Marty smiles, "I'd change my religion for something like that."

"From what I've seen, Marty, that is your religion," Danny taunts.

"Yeah, the girls do worship me, don't they?" Marty chuckles, proud of his reputation.

"It ain't what you've got, Marty," Danny grunts, "it's how you use it."

With five men short of a team, they gaze around, impatiently.

"Hey, Danny," Joe says, nodding toward a solitary spectator, "why don't you ask him if he wants to play?"

"Why don't you?" Danny replies."

"Because you're the one that's whining, that's why. I'm just in it for a giggle and a bit of fresh air."

"Do you see his glasses?" Danny asks, rhetorically. "They're as thick as friggin Coke bottles."

"Yeah, but he might have some talent, mate, which is more than you can say."

"Oh, very funny, Joe. So why am I the friggin captain?"

Joe ignores the question, and Danny jogs across the field to greet the spectator.

"Good Morning," he says, extending his hand.

"Oh, ya, guut morning," the stranger replies, with a thick accent.

"My name's Danny. What's yours?"

"I'm Hans, ya."

"You play soccer, Hans?"

"Da fuutball, oh ya. Vee play dat back ome."

"How about playing for us then? We're down a couple of guys, and could use a little help. Can you play goalie?"

"Da keeper? Oh, ya."

"Shit, that's great, Hans. Well, come on then. We'll be starting in a few minutes, and after the game we'll buy you lunch and a couple of beers."

Danny and Hans jog onto the field to join the rest, who have borrowed players from the opposing team to balance the sides. The referee exchanges greetings with Danny and the opposing captain, completes the coin toss, and whistles for the game to begin. It is immediately apparent that The Raiders are hopelessly outmatched.

Hans has placed his glasses by the goal post, and is loosening his muscles by jumping up and down and flapping his arms when he sees a blurred horde stampeding toward him. "Gott im Himmel," he exclaims, grabbing his glasses and cramming them crookedly on his face, and just in time to see the fuzzy outline of a ball streaking toward him like a meteorite. It strikes him in the stomach and collapses him like a burst balloon, and bounces away, and is kicked wide of the goal by an attacker. Danny dashes up breathlessly, and dances jubilantly over Hans.

"Jesus Christ," he hollers, "did you see that? Did you guys see that? What a goddamn save! Have we got us a goalie, or what?"

Joe runs up, and bends over Hans.

"Are you alright, lad?"

"Oh, ya," Hans gasps, smiling, and catching his breath: "Dat man shuer can boot da fuutball."

"On your feet then, lad," Joe grins, pulling Hans upright. "Are you gonna take the kick, or do you want me to?"

Hans straightens his glasses: "Oh, ya, pleeze, deeze shoes are no guut fer dat."

Joe sets the ball, and boots it deep into the other half of the field, but it is booted right back. Devin traps it, eludes a tackle, and shoots a long low pass to Cruz, who speeds down the wing looking to center the ball. Danny and Marty scramble down the middle of the field within a few feet of each other with their eyes on a Cruz, but end up colliding with each other and falling in a heap. Devin watches in amusement, and throws up his hands in mock despair.

"When will you bloody Yanks ever learn?" he bellows, dramatically.

"Hey, don't yell at us," Danny shouts. "Tell old twinkle toes Cruz to pass it sooner!"

"Yeah, that's right," Marty agrees, rubbing grass and dirt from his knees.

"Pass it? Pass it where? He had no one to pass it to, because you wankers were stuck together like Laurel and Hardy."

"Oh bullshit," Danny grumbles, kicking a tuft of grass, "he wouldn't have passed it anyway; he thinks he's David Beckham."

The game continues in a comical spectacle of miss-kicks, bad passes, bungling collisions, with players rolling on the ground giggling at their own clumsiness. Mercifully for The Raiders, time runs out, and the game ends. They congratulate the other team and straggle off the field, exhausted but happy.

"Hey, lads, look at it this way," Devin chuckles, "we're definitely getting better; we only lost by six goals this week."

"Seven, if it wasn't for old Hans," Danny adds.

"That's right," Devin agrees, turning to Hans. "Hey, Hans, how about joining us for a beer? We owe you one."

"One!" Danny exclaims. "What are we, cheap bastards? He's our goalie, isn't he? And he'll have lunch on us, and as many beers as he wants. Right Hans?"

"Oh, shuer, dat vuud be guut."

They towel-off, and pull on sweats, and Joe is the first to leave.

"I'll see you losers next week," he smiles.

"Hey, what's this then, Joe," Devin taunts, "got to rush home and do the dishes?"

"Yeah, that's right Dev. No, seriously, mate, Janie's sick again. Maybe next week. Cheerio, lads."

"I'm sorry to hear that, Joe. Give her a hug for me," Devin says, concerned.

"I will. Thanks, Dev. See ya, Danny, see ya Shawn, see ya Marty, see ya Cruz."

They shout goodbye, more or less in unison, as Joe leaves, but Shawn seems lost in his own thoughts.

"Say hello to Anna for me," Devin shouts after Joe, as he jogs toward the parking lot, "and you take care of yourself."

"I will, mate," Joe shouts, over his shoulder.

Shawn is the next to leave, excusing himself, and explaining that he's been working long hours, and wants to spend more time with his children.

"Well, that leaves us," Devin says. "Last one to the pub buys the first beer."

"Hold on, hold on," Danny exclaims struggling with his sweat pants, "what about old Hans here?"

"No problem," Marty replies, "he can ride with me, in my limo."

"He means that beat-up old van," Cruz chuckles, pointing toward a gray van at the corner of the parking lot.

"What would you know about transportation, Cruz?" Marty teases. Where you're from they're still riding on donkeys."

They make their way to the parking lot, dribbling a ball, laughing and jostling each other, and bound for a pub called The Jolly Roger.

CHAPTER TWO

The Jolly Roger is a British pub of sorts, but with a flat roof and a drop-ceiling it has none of the old-world charm of a real public house, despite photographs of the monarchy and the regalia of plastic shields, crossed swords, and the other imperial trappings of war. The name, Jolly Roger, probably derived from the dreaded red flag of pirates, known as the 'joli rouge," or even from the nickname of the devil himself, and harks back to a semi-literate world of signs and icons. But this would be of little interest to The Raiders, who have imbued the pub with their own identity, and regard it as a home away from home, which they fondly refer to as The Roger. The owner is Sally, a young Irish woman who has done her best to serve authentic food, including cucumber and watercress sandwiches and other unique dishes, such as fish-and-chips, steak-and-kidney pie, toad-in-the-hole, and bangers-and-mash, all served with beer and ale, jiggers of Irish whiskey, soft drinks, and seasonal hot toddies.

Devin, Cruz, Marty, Danny, and Hans enter the pub and pause while their eyes adjust from the brilliant sunlight to the shadowy world within. Danny and Marty greet some regulars at the bar and then slip into their favorite booth, where Sally soon joins them to take their order.

"What will it be then, lads?" she asks.

Sally is an intelligent and fiercely independent woman, who could hold her own with any man. She has rosy cheeks, copper colored hair, and voluptuous breasts. To The Raiders, she is the lady of the house, the one who must be obeyed, and reminds them, perhaps at an subconscious level, of the great earth-mother and of a time when the world was matriarchal and the White Goddess of birth, love, and death reigned supreme in the night sky, a time when life was tied to the seasons and nature was revered.

"Well, let's see, darling," Danny replies, savoring her presence while pretending to decide. "What shall we have, today?" he smiles. "Yes, that's it; we'll have a tall glass of fresh-squeezed lemonade, two small milks, one hot chocolate, a piping hot cup of English tea, and a photograph of a bacon sandwich."

"Very funny, Danny. Now, one more time, what will it be, or you can find someone else to serve you?"

"Alright, sweetheart, bring us five Boddingtons, five bacon sandwiches, and a large order of what we real Americans call french-fries."

Sally is about to leave, when Marty catches her arm. "Hey, Sal, where's that new waitress? You know, the young Welsh one with the, ugh, well, you know, the big green eyes," he says with a wink, raising his hands as though holding melons.

"If you must know, Marty, she quit right after you starting ogling her."

"Oh, come on Sal, you can't be serious. She fancied me, I know she did."

"Tell him, would you, boys? Someone has to."

"Tell me what, that you're mad with jealousy, and frightened of losing me?"

"That's right, love, dream on," she chuckles, shaking her head. "You're a right case, you are, Marty, but I do love you."

"Don't say that, Sal," Danny laments, "you'll break my heart."

"You're special too, love," Sally replies, "and don't you ever forget it."

"Thanks, Sal. You're the only one for me. You know that, don't you?" he winks.

While they wait for their food, they engage in casual conversation.

"So what's up with Joe's little girl," Cruz asks, "the flue?"

"No, unfortunately, it's serious," Danny says. "She had leukemia a year ago, and it's come back, and she's in hospital again, but Joe doesn't like to talk about it."

"You can understand that; leukemia's a scary word."

"No shit," Marty agrees.

"Oh, man, how do you explain that to a child?" Cruz wonders out loud.

"Oh, she knows," Danny says. "She's really sharp."

"So how are they managing?" Cruz asks Danny.

"Well, Anna quit her job, and she's practically living at the hospital. But it has been messing with both of them, big time. Joe's not eating, and he must have lost fifteen pounds in the last couple of weeks. You can see the despair in his eyes. I wish there was something we could all do," he adds, wistfully, "but there's nothing we can do."

"Do they have insurance, at least?" Cruz asks.

"Yeah," Danny acknowledges, "but it ain't worth a damn."

"Ain't that a bitch?" Marty exclaims.

"So how are they managing?" Cruz asks again.

"You know how it is," Danny explains. "They're hanging in there, using what little they've managed to save, and doing the best they can."

Unsure of what else to say, they look around in silence until Sally returns with their beers.

"Thanks, love," Devin says, as she places the beers before them.

Danny tries to change the subject. "So, Hans," he blurts out, "what brings you to America, business or pleasure?"

"Oh, ya," Hans replies.

"Oh, ya, what?" Danny replies, mimicking his idiom.

"Oh, ya, der beezness and der pleazure, ya. I cum fer der oliday, buy der used golf balls, den I zell dem back ome, ya, and make der oliday and der monies. Iz guut, ya?"

Danny is fascinated. "Yeah, I guess," he agrees. "So what you're telling us is that you come over here for a vacation, buy a bunch of friggin golf balls, ship em back home, clean em up, I suppose, and then sell em again. Is that how it works?"

"Oh, ya. Iz guut, ya?"

"If you say so, man. So, how much money can you make doing that?"

"It depenz, ya? Tuu, maybe tree-touzan."

"Dollars?" Danny gasps.

"Oh, ya," Hans beams.

"Jesus! And you don't even get dirty."

"Oh, ya," Hans smiles, starting to feel at home among his new companions.

"Well, boys, here's to old Hans," Danny says, raising his glass. "He's a regular goddamned capitalist," he adds grinning, "and we could learn a thing or two from him, ya?"

"Where are you from?" Cruz asks.

"Frum Germany, ya, da Deutschland, unt Olland, ya, but I luv der Merica, unt I vud cum to leeve if I cuud."

"So how long are you staying?" Marty asks.

"Tu, tree veeks, maybe leetle longer."

"Oh, yeah, and what do you do back home?"

"I study fer der law, ya."

"You do?" Danny questions. "That's funny, because you don't act like a prick."

"Vos dat, der preek?"

"Ah, it's nothing, mate," Devin explains, "Danny's just kidding. He's not too fond of lawyers. One of them ripped him off on a plumbing job, and he thinks they're all, well, you know, pricks," he grins, pointing to his crotch.

"So, Hans, do you have a woman back home in Holland?" Marty asks.

"I yuuzed to, ya, but she marry der lawyer; der preek, ya."

"What a bitch," Marty exclaims, but his comment is lost in laughter.

They discuss ways of improving their soccer game, while they enjoy their refreshments, and then arrange to meet for practice later in the week.

CHAPTER THREE

Shawn is making sandwiches in a state-of-the-art kitchen. His children are seated at a large granite-topped island when his wife, Helen, enters. He greets her with a smile, but she is too preoccupied to notice. She kisses the children, and then rummages through a drawer.

"I'll see you kids later," she says, "and don't forget to clean your rooms before you go out to play."

"Where are you going, all dolled up?" Shawn asks.

"Work," she replies, bluntly.

"What, dressed like that? I thought the office was closed on weekends."

"It is, but I've got work to do. Talking about work, isn't that what you're supposed to be doing?"

"I can't. I poured a bunch of footings yesterday, and I have to wait until later this afternoon before I can remove the forms."

"You mean you've only got one job going?" she asks.

"Yeah, you know how it is in winter," he replies. "There's a lot of competition out there," he adds. "Besides, you don't have to be a rocket scientist to pound nails."

She turns to face him, with her hands planted on her hips:

"And you really don't have to explain that to me," she says, sarcastically.

The words hurt, as she had intended; pain as punishment.

"What are you looking for anyway?" he asks, dejectedly.

"Nothing," she replies, curtly, and turns and walks out of the kitchen.

Shawn hesitates, encourages the children to finish eating, by promising to take them on a hike in the hills as soon as they're finished, and follows Helen upstairs. She is seated on their bed, putting on some new, red high-heeled shoes, but stands as he enters and contemplates her reflection in a full-length mirror.

"I need money," she states, bluntly.

He pulls out his wallet, removes two tens, and hands them to her.

"I need more than that."

"It's all I've got on me. What do you need it for, anyway?"

"I'm going out with the girls, later, and my Visa's maxed."

"You mean everyone's working?"

"No, I'm meeting them later, at a restaurant."

"Does that mean you won't be eating with us, tonight?"

"Isn't that obvious?"

"Yeah, I guess it is," he exclaims, angrily, and I guess it explains the new fuck-me shoes, as well."

"You're disgusting, you know that?" she sneers.

He exhales, and lowers his head.

"You're right," he admits. "I shouldn't have said that. It was wrong, and spiteful, and I'm sorry. But why the hell are we letting this happen to us?"

She ignores the question, stuffs the bills into a cocktail purse, checks her reflection once more, and walks out of the bedroom.

"You look beautiful," he adds, wistfully. But she ignores him and walks on down the stairs. He hesitates, but continues to talk to her as she descends the curved staircase.

"So, we're not going to talk about it?"

"Talk about what?"

"About us, about what's happening to us. You're hardly ever home, I'm doing most of the cooking and cleaning, and you don't even seem to want to spend time with the kids."

"That's because you don't make enough money to pay the bills."

"We were doing just fine, Helen, until you insisted on buying this colossus."

She turns and glares at him without speaking, and then stands shaking her head.

"I don't know what I ever saw in you," she says, disdainfully.

"What is it, another man? Is that what it is?"

She turns and walks away toward the garage, as he continues to plead with her.

"Hey, Helen, I'm sorry. Can't we talk about this?"

She disappears into the garage and, as he stands listening, he hears her car start, the garage door opening and closing, and the sound of the engine fading in the distance. He rubs his face dejectedly, and then hurries down the stairs and into the kitchen.

"Hey, Dad," his daughter says.

"Yeah, what is it, darling?" he replies with feigned enthusiasm.

"Doesn't Mom want to be with us anymore?"

"Are you kidding?" he grins. "Of course she does. She has work to do, that's all."

"But she didn't even say goodbye."

"Yes, she did, she gave you both a kiss. Remember?"

"Yes, but she didn't say goodbye; she just left."

"Oh, that doesn't mean anything. She's just mad at me. That's all."

"But, Dad, if you and Mom stop loving each other," she persists, "will you separate, like Ryan's parents?"

"Are you kidding? We're a family, and families stick together. Now, come on," he adds, enthusiastically, "we've got to get going if we're gonna hike; I've got to drop you off at Grandma's in a couple of hours, so I can get back to work."

Several hours later, Shawn is alone on a hillside behind a mansion in the Trousdale Estates overlooking Los Angeles where distant skyscrapers loom through a blanket of smog. He is wearing nail-bags and removing forms from a series of footings on which a cantilevered redwood deck will be built. He slips his framing-hammer back into his nail-bags, scrambles up the hill, climbs into his truck, and sits for several minutes, lost in thought. Finally, after checking his watch several times, he drives away.

After twenty minutes or so, he pulls over to the edge of the road and stares across an almost empty parking lot at two cars parked in front of a tall building, one of which belongs to Helen. He rolls his head, and rubs his neck, as if trying to dispel a headache, and is about to start the truck and drive away when he sees Helen coming out of the building with a man. He watches as the man opens the door of a Jaguar for her and then settles in behind the wheel, but they remain parked. Shawn stares blankly as their silhouettes merge in an embrace. He sits, stunned for a moment, and then starts the truck, pulls into the lot, parks across the back of the car, jumps out, jerks the passenger door open, and confronts Helen.

"So I'm disgusting, am I? Well, I must be some sort of a fool as well, because I never thought you'd sink this low. And I guess this mannequin is your idea of a man, or is it just his money that excites you?"

"Now, look here ..." the man protests.

"You keep your mouth shut," Shawn snaps, through clenched teeth, "I've got no quarrel with you, but one more word and I'll drag you out of there and kick your ass."

Shawn glares at him, hoping that he'll accept the challenge so that he can vent his rage, but the man remains silent, and Shawn feels suddenly weak and helpless. He turns to Helen, swallows hard, and delivers an ultimatum:

"I'll give you ten days to file for a divorce, and then I will. I'm taking the kids, my clothes, my tools, and the truck. You can see the kids whenever you want, and the house, the furniture, the car, and everything else is yours, including what's left in savings. You've got your own salary, and you'd better learn to live on it."

Leaving the car door open, he turns and walks back to his truck, feeling the darkness closing in. He starts the engine and drives slowly out of the parking lot, the only movement on a desolate expanse of asphalt.

CHAPTER FOUR

Ventura Boulevard is one of the oldest continuously traveled routes through the valley, and part of what is known as El Camino Real, or the Royal Highway, on which a chain of twenty-one missions was established by the Spanish, throughout California. But, apart from a few arrowheads and musket balls in private collections, there is little left to tell of its role in imperial history. But when the sun sets and the moon rises, and the lights flicker on, it is transformed from a congested and smoggy traffic-corridor into a glittering strand of five-star restaurants, featuring the haute cuisine of many cultures. This is where Devin and Cruz spend six evenings a week catering to the public in Giuseppe's old-world Italian restaurant, which has been in the same family for seventy years. Inside the restaurant Maurice, the head-waiter and part-time maitre d', escorts a couple to a secluded table-for-two, and stands holding the chair for the woman.

"Madam," he smiles, bowing his head.

The woman is young, and somewhat intimated by the deferential treatment. Her companion is much older, arrogant, and ill-mannered. Maurice hands them menus and a wine list, and returns to his station in the foyer.

Light classical music mingles with the murmur of intimate conversations. Beyond a set of swinging doors, and off a corridor that leads to the back of the restaurant, the kitchen is a startling contrast to the romantic world of the dining room. It is a mechanical world of white light, which accentuates the glint of stainless steel, the roar and smell of smoke and flame and the hiss of steam, in which uniformed figures scurry back and forth like white mice. Devin and Cruz enter, and wait by a warming shelf on which entrées are lined up. They look elegant in tailored tuxedos; emissaries from the romantic world of the dining room. As soon as two entrées are placed on the shelf in front of him, Devin grabs them, returns to the dining room, and places them carefully in front of a young couple. He is conversing politely with them when he feels a tug at his tuxedo, and turns to see the couple that Maurice had just seated.

"One moment, sir, and I'll be right with you," he says, feigning a smile. But, the man is insistent.

"Send the maitre d' over here, now," he adds, with emphasis.

"Yes, sir, of course. One moment, please."

"I said, now," the man repeats. "And I mean now," he adds, becoming belligerent.

Devin excuses himself, leaves the table, and signals for Maurice, who is aware that an angry voice has sent a discordant tone through the harmony of the room, and quickly joins Devin in the shadows, where they stand conferring.

"The guy on table eight wants to see you, and he's pissed-off about something."

Devin returns to the kitchen, and is waiting at the warming shelf for other entrées when Maurice appears.

"What the hell's going on?" he demands. "He says he's been waiting for ten minutes."

"Well, that's nonsense, isn't it? You seated them yourself. It couldn't have been more than four or five minutes, at the most; hardly time for him to look at the bloody menu, let alone the wine list."

"Well, get over there and kiss his ass."

"I'm sorry, Maurice," Devin grins, "I just can't bring myself to do that. But I'll kiss his girlfriend's ass if you could arrange that for me."

"Stop acting like an idiot; I thought you English were supposed to be cultured. Now get back over there and kiss his ass, before he makes another scene."

Devin sighs, and returns to the table.

"Good evening sir, madam. Would you care for a glass of wine or a cocktail, before dinner?"

The man glares at him, over reading glasses.

"Oh, it's you. Yes, we would, if that's not asking too much."

"Not at all, sir. It will be my pleasure to serve you," Devin replies.

"That's better," the man says, jabbing him in the stomach with the wine list.

"Thank you, sir," Devin says, accepting it, and smiling with artificial sweetness.

"I'll take a bottle of your Mondovi Chardonnay," the man grunts.

"Certainly, sir. And, will that be one or two glasses?" Devin smiles, intending to irk him.

"One or two glasses?" the man splutters. "Two damn glasses of course. What do you think I meant?"

"I'm sorry, sir, but you did say 'I'll take a bottle,' and madam does look remarkably young, young enough to be your daughter even. And, of course, we have to be so very careful these days."

The man is about to explode, when the woman reaches across the table and grabs his hand.

"Arni, please," she implores, but the man jerks his hand away.

"Just bring the damn wine! Haven't you wasted enough of our time?"

Devin nods, and leaves, but the man shouts after him:

"And bring us some Bruschetta!"

An elderly man at an adjoining table stares reprovingly at him, but is stared down. The woman leans across the table, imploring him:

"Arni, please, if you're going to start shouting like you do at the office you can take me home."

"Why don't you mind your own damn business?" he snaps.

"For God's sake, Arni, you don't have to be that way."

"Apparently, I do," he snarls.

Devin emerges from a basement wine cellar polishing a bottle and encounters Cruz, who is on his way to the kitchen.

"Hey, Cruz, do you have a gun I can borrow?" he jests.

"Why, what's up?"

"Oh, just some rich twit trying to impress his young girlfriend. You know how that is."

"Do you want to switch stations?" Cruz asks.

"No, that would probably piss him off even more. Thanks anyway, but I sure am tired of serving rich pigs."

"I know what you mean," Cruz agrees.

"I guess I'll just have to grin and bear it," Devin adds.

"That's right," Cruz nods, "unless you're lucky enough to win the lottery."

"The opiate of the masses," Devin grins. "Wouldn't that be nice?"

Resigned to his subservient role, he returns purposefully to the table.

"Here you are, sir," he says, feigning a smile. "A wise choice, indeed."

The man nods, and Devin pours a dash of wine into his glass, and waits until he grunts his approval. Then, he pours a glass for the woman and fills the man's glass.

"I'll be right back with your appetizer," he adds, leaving the table.

The man stares after him until he is out of earshot, and then leans across the table and whispers to the woman.

"So, are we on for tonight, or what?"

"I've already told you, Arni, I'm not like that."

"Not like what, for Christ's sake?"

"You know what I mean."

"Look, we spend the night at my place and get to know each other a little better. What's so wrong with that?"

"I've already told you, I'm not that type of girl."

"And I'm not that type of guy. All I'm trying to say is …."

Devin returns with the appetizer, interrupting them, and places it on the table.

"Here you are folks. Enjoy."

The man glares at Devin until he leaves, and continues to badger the woman.

A short time later, when Devin returns to the kitchen to pick up their entrées he notices Cruz rearranging the vegetables on one of them with a fork. What he doesn't notice is that Cruz has positioned two pearl onions and a baby carrot to resemble an erect phallus.

"Look, I customized his entrée," Cruz announces, proudly. Devin looks but doesn't see anything, until Cruz turns the plate to present a slightly different angle.

"Oh, shit," Devin snorts, recognizing Cruz's handiwork, "if he sees that, I'll be fired for sure. Giuseppe's already pissed because I haven't got a haircut, yet."

"He probably won't even notice. You didn't," Cruz reminds him.

"Yeah, but what if he does?"

"So, you turn it the other way, and let his girlfriend get the message. Go ahead, she'll probably enjoy it."

"Sure why not. It'll be good for giggle, I suppose. Hey, you didn't do anything else to it, did you?"

"No, of course not," Cruz assures him.

Devin returns to the table, and places the woman's entrée in front of her.

"There you are, madam," he says, holding her entrée with a serviette and placing it carefully in front of her. "And, there you are, sir," he says, placing the other entrée in front of the man, and turning it slightly, while glancing at the woman. "Be careful now, the plates are very hot. Enjoy."

Cruz stands at the edge of the room with his hands clasped, expressionless, and watches as Devin places the entrées on the table and leaves. But, Devin is only a few steps away from the table when the man shouts: "Waiter! Waiter!"

"Sir," Devin replies, returning immediately.

"What's this?"

"Excuse me, sir?"

"I said, 'what's this?'"

"Why, that's what you ordered, sir, one of the house specials: Salmon in a Dijon-mustard sauce."

"I know that you idiot," the man snarls. "I mean that, that, that," he repeats, stabbing his finger at the tiny effigy.

"That's garlic-mashed potatoes with vegetables. It comes with the meal, sir."

The man levels a trembling finger at the effigy.

"Are you telling me that you didn't deliberately arrange that?"

Devin glances at the woman, who is covering her mouth to conceal a smile.

"I'm sorry, sir, I have no idea what you're talking about."

The man jumps up, bunches his napkin, and throws it on the table. Cruz slips out of the dining room through the swinging doors and into the kitchen, smothering his laughter, while Devin stands motionless, feigning astonishment. The man shoves him to one side, grabs the woman, and pushes her through the dining room and out into the foyer, where Maurice stands anticipating an assault.

"You haven't heard the last of this," the man shouts. "I'm going to report this restaurant to the Better Business Bureau. And, if you know what's good for you you'll fire that goddamned waiter immediately!"

"But, sir, what happened?" Maurice asks, wringing his hands as a hush falls over the dining room. The man ignores the question, and continues to push the woman out of the restaurant. Maurice considers following him, but glancing back at the table and seeing Devin carrying the entrées back to the kitchen, he hurries across the dining room, through the swinging doors, and into Giuseppe's office.

Devin sets the entrées on a side table, leans against a wall and sighs. A moment later, the doors fly open and Giuseppe appears with Maurice, a silent witness. All activity in the kitchen stops. Devin remains leaning against a wall with his head back and his eyes closed, while Cruz remains doubled over in silent laughter, pointing at him. Giuseppe looks from one to the other, but shouts at Devin.

"Alright, whadda de hellza goin on?"

"Don't ask me to explain, boss, because I can't. I served this prick--excuse me--I served this customer what he ordered, which was one of the specials, and he went ballistic on me."

Hearing the customer referred to a prick sends Cruz into another convulsion of silent laughter, but he nods in agreement. Giuseppe glares at him in disgust, and then lifts the entrée and studies it. He pokes the fish with his finger, and then with his eyes flicking from Devin to Cruz he raises it slowly to his nose and sniffs.

"Youdda beta tella me de truth," he warns, "you putta sometink in hiza dinner?"

"Of course I didn't," Devin protests. "What do you take me for? If you don't believe me, ask Maurice. The guy's a bloody nut-case!"

"So whazzee laughin at?" Giuseppe screams, nodding at Cruz.

"How should I know?" Devin protests. "Why don't you ask him?"

Giuseppe puts the entrée down, glares suspiciously at both of them, but gives up.

"Getta backa t'work. Neitha one of youze iza wortha shit. If I hadda da sense, I'da fire da boat of youze. Anna getta goddamn haircut, for Christ's sake!" he shouts, even louder.

The kitchen staff remains motionless, staring at the little drama.

"Whadda da hella youze staring at," Giuseppe explodes. "Whadda ya tinka we're doin here, running da god-damned strip-joint? Getta backa to work or I'll fire evera one of youze," he threatens as the kitchen erupts in a renewed frenzy of activity.

Later that evening, when the restaurant is closed, Devin and Cruz are seated in a staff lounge adjacent to Giuseppe's office sipping coffee, with their bow-ties off and their jackets open, while Giuseppe is sitting in his office on the opposite side of the corridor with the door ajar, tallying the evening's receipts. Cruz is just a teenager, who got his job as a waiter through Devin, and only because Devin exaggerated not only his age but his qualifications. But Cruz is very intelligent and a keen student, and has quickly earned the respect of Giuseppe and the staff.

"Well, Dev, another day another dollar," Cruz smiles.

"You've got that right. Damn, I hate serving rich people."

"Me too, but what else can we do? One way or another, we'd be serving somebody."

"Well, I don't know about you, but I sure wish I could chuck it all in and go back to merry old England."

"So what bought you over here?" Cruz asks.

"Oh, I dunno, it's complicated. I grew up thinking that the Brits owned the whole bloody world, that they were special, and had a glorious history, you know, that sort of thing. And then I realized that that was only one way of looking at it; and in another way they were plunderers and murderers, and I guess I was looking for something, something different, and I thought I might find it here, in America. Anyway, I thought I'd give it a try for awhile. You know how it is when you're young. But I always believed I'd end up back in England. Then I met Laurie and that was it. I was captured. And now I'm a prisoner of love," he grins.

"You're a lucky man, that's what you are," Cruz asserts.

"I am. I'm truly blessed," Devin adds, grinning.

"But what about you, Cruz, what brought you to the land-of-the-free and the home-of-the-brave? Were you looking for something, too, or was it just the money?"

"Neither. Oh, I dunno, maybe both."

"So, tell me."

"Nah, it's a long story."

"So give me the short version."

"I really don't like talking about the past."

"Ah, come on, Cruz, I've told you my whole life's story, for Christ's sake."

"Yeah, but mine's not that interesting."

"So tell me anyway," Devin insists, "I know you're smart and a good soccer player, but apart from that I hardly know anything about you."

"What do you want to know?" Cruz asks, fidgeting self-consciously.

"Anything: where you lived, what you did, your family, that sort of thing."

"Well, there were four of us back in El Salvador, in a place called Chalatenango: my father, my mother, and my younger brother, Antonio. We had a small farm: not much; a few cows, goats, that sort of thing, but enough to keep us in food, with a little left over to sell at the market. And, believe it or not, I had a scholarship to study medicine. In fact, my family counted on me becoming a doctor, and had their hopes pinned on me."

"Man, that's impressive, but I always knew you were smart; perfect English, and all," Devin smiles.

"Anyway", Cruz continues, "my father got sick, real sick, inoperable cancer, and we lost him, and just about everything else as well."

"Jesus, Cruz, I'm sorry I asked."

"That's okay, Dev. It's probably better for me to talk about it. Anyway," he continues, "we had to give up the farm and move to the city, where my mother got a job cleaning offices. But it didn't pay much, and most of the time we just squeaked by. Then one morning when she was serving us breakfast my brother asked her why she wasn't eating, and she said that she'd eaten before we got up. But it was a lie, and he knew it, knew that there wasn't even enough food for the three of us, and that she was going hungry for us, and he became hysterical.

What with our dad dying and our mother going without food, it was more than he could take, and he sort of went crazy, cursing God and screaming at my mother for lying. And, the truth is, he'd never cursed before, never talked back, or even raised his voice. Then, all of a sudden, he burst into tears. And pretty soon my mother was crying, and I was crying, and you might even say it was the day our family died. Anyway, when it was all over, we hugged each other and my mother left for work. That night in bed, I could hear my brother crying softly, but when I asked about it he told me to shut-up and go to sleep. Then, when we got up the next morning he was gone. He left a note telling us not to worry, and that he was going to find work and send us money."

Cruz lowers his head and seems lost in thought, while Devin searches in vain for some words of comfort.

"I don't know what to say, mate," Devin says, regretting that he'd been so insistent.

"There's nothing to say," Cruz allows.

"So, how old was he?" Devin asks.

"Sixteen," Cruz mutters, without raising his head.

"Jesus, that's awfully young to be out on your own."

"Yeah, it is," Cruz agrees, perking up a little, "but he made it, made it all the way to the States. And before long he was sending more money in a week than my mother was making in a month. It was really something. Every night, my mother would kneel down and repeat the same prayer: 'Bless my son, Antonio, dear Lord, and bless America and her children.' The truth is he was sending us hope."

"Wow, that's something. So how long after that before you and your mother came over here?"

"Well, we squirreled away every dime until we had enough money to travel to Mexico and buy our way across the border, but when we got here, we learned that he'd been killed."

"Oh, my God. What happened?"

"We don't know. We got different stories from the police on both sides of the border, and I don't think we'll ever know the whole truth. But it seems he'd been beaten pretty badly in Mexico and then dumped just across the border in the States, and left there to die. His pockets were turned inside out, his shirt and shoes were gone, and his crucifix had been ripped from his neck."

"Good Lord, Cruz, are you saying that he was murdered for the clothes on his back?"

"That, and whatever money he had. Life is cheap in Mexico."

"I'm sorry I asked, mate," Devin says, lowering his head.

"That's alright," Cruz smiles, wryly, "I still get choked up when I think of him, but his death crippled my mother. All she does now is pray, but as if she's actually talking to God. And when she's not praying, she tells anyone that will listen that the Devil lives in America, and that all she really wants is to take his body back to Chalatenango and bury him on the farm. And I just don't have the heart to tell her that we spent most of what he sent us getting here and the rest on his funeral and trying to find out what happened to him. So that's it, for a year or two," Cruz adds. "We're stuck here, in the land-of-the-free. But, the truth is money makes slaves of us all," he smiles, trying to change the subject, "and none of us are ever really free, or maybe just once when we're children."

"My God, Cruz, what keeps you going?"

"I guess I've never thought about it. I guess I just keep on keeping on. I believe in God, I suppose. I mean, I'm a Catholic, but I only go to church to please my mother."

"You mean you believe in the Devil and stuff like that?"

"No, not really. But how about you, what keeps you going, Dev? What do you believe in?"

"I'm not sure either. I guess you'd say I'm agnostic."

"I forget what that means," Cruz says.

"Well, it means that you'd be willing to believe if someone could convince you that there's something to believe in."

"So you're not an atheist, then?"

"Oh, hell, no, it's just that I have a hard time believing in the supernatural. You know, believing that some bloke could walk on water, or raise the dead, or feed hundreds of people with a couple of loaves of barley bread. You know what I mean?"

"Yes, I do, but I really don't think about it that much, do you?"

"Yeah, I do. I honestly do. And I used to think about it a lot when I was kid, in England, and it scared the beejezus out of me. Then, one day when I was sitting on the beach and looking out over the waves, it occurred to me that maybe we had it wrong and that we were never meant to believe in stuff like that. You know what I mean, some bloke walking on the water and raising the dead? And maybe people were just trying to make a point about people who were really special. You see what I'm getting at?"

"No, I can't say that I do, Dev."

"Well, look at it like this. Perhaps they really didn't mean that Jesus actually walked on the water, they meant that he was, well, you know, a very special person."

"Then why didn't they just come out and say it?"

"Well, they did in a way, when they talked about someone who could change water into wine. But they didn't mean it, literally. It was just their way of saying it."

"I'm still not sure what you mean."

"Alright, okay, look at it this way. Supposing I told you that Danny could eat a horse, you wouldn't believe that, would you?"

"Are you kidding, of course I would? I know darn well he could."

"No, look, what I really mean is you'd understand that I just meant that he has a big appetite, right, not that he would literally eat a horse?"

"Oh, I see," Cruz nods, "I get it now. That's interesting. In other words, they didn't really expect us to believe that Jesus actually walked upon the water, but that he was a special individual, and that was just their way of expressing it."

"Exactly," Devin exclaims eagerly. "Jesus was really someone special, like Gandhi, and Martin Luther King. You know what I mean?"

"I do, I do," Cruz agrees, enthusiastically. "It was sort of like they were making pictures with words."

"That's exactly right," Devin grins. And that's probably the way things were, a long time ago. I mean, look at it like this. Not too long ago, right here in America, the Indians believed that the earth was their mother, and that's why they refused to sit on chairs, or wear shoes, and be separated from her. And they went absolutely berserk when the settlers strung out barbed-wire and drove stakes into what they believed was their mother's breast. And maybe that's not so crazy after all. Just look at what we've done to the earth in the last three-hundred years."

"That's an interesting way to think about religion, but you'd never get people like my mother to believe that," Cruz adds.

"Probably not," Devin agrees. "The truth is that most people would rather kill each other than change their religious beliefs. But it sort of makes sense to me."

"So, what do you believe in then?" Cruz asks.

"I guess just about everything that men haven't mucked with yet; you know trees, birds, fish, flowers, the moon and the stars, animals. That's what's sacred as far as I'm concerned, things that are eternal, things that are still a mystery."

"And that makes sense, too," Cruz allows.

"But you know what else," Devin continues, "and this is going to sound corny, but I believe in love. I love my mother and my father, and Laurie, and my mates, and I'm certainly going to love my child, and I even love England. And, God knows, I'll probably end up loving America as well. Love is something that needs time to grow, if you know what I mean?"

"Yes, I do, I absolutely do, because everyone needs something to believe in. Take Marty, for instance," he grins, "There's a guy who really believes in love. Right?"

"He certainly does," Devin agrees.

They would have continued talking, but are interrupted by a shout from Giuseppe, who is seated at his desk sorting stacks of bills into their denominations.

"Hey, one a youze out dere, bring me another Spresso!"

"Coming right up, boss-man," Devin replies, jumping up and winking at Cruz.

CHAPTER FIVE

Marty is a computer salesman who has never owned one, or wanted to, believing in a way that he finds hard to put into words that they provide an empty experience, or one that does not involve the senses, or provide any real sustenance; a nutrition of consciousness. But his friends pay little attention to what he says, and tend to regard him merely as a lady's man. But he's not; he's much too gentle, and not in the least narcissistic. However, his pursuit of the ladies, has kept him penniless, which is why at twenty-eight he still lives in bachelor's quarters above a garage, in his parent's modest home in Valley Village.

There is an child-like innocence about Marty, which endears him to most people, but which has left him somewhat neurotic, a condition most evident in private moments. Dressed for a dinner-date, in a suit that was bought for him by his parents as a graduation present, he contemplates his image in a full-length mirror. The suit is too tight and accentuates the weight that he has gained over the years. But, as he continues to stare, he slips into a reverie and sees only an idealized image of himself. Younger, and twenty pounds lighter, he steps through the looking-glass into an imaginary nightclub where a female fantasy awaits. He strolls over to her table, smiling confidently.

"Well, hello there, miss. And how are you, this lovely evening?"

"I'm fine, thank you, sir," she replies, lowering her eyes, modestly.

"Yes, you certainly are," he grins. "What d'ya say we show these locals a few moves?"

She stands, pouts her lips, and extends her hand, which Marty takes and leads her onto the center of an empty dance floor, where they dazzle onlookers with a sensuous tango until the muffled ring of a telephone shatters Marty's reverie. He fumbles among the covers of his unmade bed, and finds the phone.

"Oh, Hi, Ma. Shoot. I forgot to mention that I'm eating out tonight," he explains. "Got a date with a dream. Yeah, of course I will. You take care, too. Okay, see ya sometime tomorrow. Love ya, Ma."

He hangs up the telephone, stares into the mirror, brushes his hair back, composes himself, and steps through the looking-glass and into the nightclub. Only this time his fantasy is more mundane. His weight is real, and the once provocative female is now lounging in a chair, smoking.

"Why, hello again, little lady. What d'ya say we take up where we left off?"

She looks up, and blows smoke in his face.

"What d'ya say you get lost, before my boyfriend comes back and kicks your fat ass?"

Marty stares at his mirror-image, pinches a roll of fat around his middle, and frowns. But, then a smile creeps over his face as he slips into an amateur imitation of Robert Dinerro's celebrated character in the movie, Taxi Driver.

He turns, as if to walk away, but looks back and levels an accusatory finger at the fantasy girl's imaginary boyfriend:

"Are you talkin to me? Are you talkin to me?"

He smirks, picks up a paint pistol from a dresser, shoves it in his waistband, poses himself, and resumes the charade, but with more conviction.

"Are you talkin to me? Are you friggin talkin to me?" he repeats, more animated.

He jerks the pistol out of his waistband and points it at the mirror.

"Yeah, that's right. Ya see this?" he smirks, twirling the pistol on his finger: "You still wanna mess with me?"

He stuffs the pistol back in his waistband, and stands with his hands on his hips, grinning.

"Alright, let's see what you've got. Make your move, dick-head."

He attempts another quick-draw, but rips the waistband out of his pants.

"Oy-vay, now look what you've done," he complains to the grinning image.

He unzips his pants and hops back and forth on one leg, trying to remove them without taking off his shoes. But he becomes entangled and collapses in a heap, shredding his pants in the process.

"This isn't funny, you know," he says, lecturing the image from the floor:

"When are you gonna grow up and start acting like a man?"

CHAPTER SIX

In a children's hospital, below a cloverleaf of freeways, Joe is sitting on the edge of a planter bed in a foyer, hunched over with his face in his hands. He has been crying, and looks up as Danny returns with some tissues. Danny sits next to him, and hands them to him.

"Thanks mate," Joe says, blowing his nose and wiping his eyes. He remains seated with his lips pressed together, staring at the floor, until Danny slides closer and nudges him.

"She'll be alright, Joe, you'll see."

"I know, I know," Joe replies, swallowing hard. "It's just that …. I mean, how much can a little girl take?"

"She's a scrapper, Joe, same as you. She's done it before, and she'll do it again."

"Yeah, you're right. She will," Joe agrees.

He stands, and composes himself.

"So, do I look alright?"

"Well, you ain't exactly good-looking, mate," Danny replies, mimicking Joe's idiom. "Now piss-off, and tell Anna that I'm waiting to take her to supper."

"You're a good man, Danny," Joe mutters.

"Hey, what are friends for?"

"Yeah, I suppose so," Joe nods, and walks away.

Danny was given the birth name Daniel, after the biblical prophet, and although he was never given any religious training, he is best described in New Testament terms as the "salt of the earth." He never even knew his parents, but often wondered if he looked like his father, and fantasized about meeting him one day, face to face. And once, when he had finished shaving, he stood in front of the mirror and mouthed the word, "father," to see how it would feel to say it. But it made him silly to say it, and he never said it again.

He was born out of wedlock in Philadelphia to a young Polish immigrant, and immediately delivered to a Catholic orphanage where he spent the first year of his life. He was a happy child, or so one of the sisters told his adopted parents when they came to pick him up on his first birthday. His adoptive father worked as a bus driver for the Metropolitan Transit District in Los Angeles, while his mother kept house. But, as fate would have it, he was abandoned by them five years later, and only a few days after his sixth birthday.

Both parents were alcoholics, not in the sense of being falling-down-drunks but in being more or less permanently inebriated, or wet with alcohol. His father drove through his shifts in an alcohol-induced haze, which was particularly apparent on the late shifts. So it came as no great surprise to his fellow drivers to learn that when returning his empty bus to the depot one night he drove it into the Department of Building and Safety on Van Nuys Boulevard, a building that is no longer there, due in large measure to the structural damage caused by the bus. He was reported to have died instantly, and purportedly with a smile on his face; a fact that does not appear in the coroner's report. With meager savings, and only a small pension, his mother sank into an alcoholic depression that resulted in Danny being rescued by the Department of Social Welfare and placed in foster care. Contrary to what might be expected, Danny matured into a reasonably well-adjusted and happy adult; although it could be argued, by those who are said to understand such things, that he is still looking for love.

Joe leaves Danny in the foyer, and tip-toes into a small room at the end of a corridor, lit by the sallow light from a muted television screen. His daughter, Janie, is asleep in an elevated bed, with tubes trailing from her body. She has a serene look on her face, like that of a porcelain doll. His wife, Anna, is resting with her head on the bed, gazing at Janie, and holding one of her hands. Anna is a delicately beautiful woman, made even more delicate by the burden of her sorrow. She looks up when Joe enters and smiles. He puts his arm around her, and kisses her.

"Time to get your supper, love. Danny's waiting."

"That's alright, dear, I'm not hungry."

"Now, come on, love, you need to keep your strength up."

"I know, dear, but I really …"

"Anna," he interrupts, "you know what we promised the doctor. We've got to stay strong, for Janie. Now, get going, sweetheart, Danny's waiting for you."

Anna releases Janie's hand, stands, and embraces Joe. She appears even more delicate beside him. And, although he is ex-military, tough and sinewy, she is much stronger; an abiding force, like water. He turns away, so that she cannot see the fear in his eyes, but when she is gone he gazes at Janie for a moment and then drops to his knees and prays.

"Dear God, she's just a baby. Don't take her from us, I beg you."

He buries his face in the side of the bed to muffle his sobs. A nurse appears, silhouetted in the doorway behind him, hesitates, and leaves. Forty minutes later, Anna returns, weary, but smiling, bravely.

"Time for you to leave, sweetheart; it's a workday tomorrow."

"I'm fine, love, and I'm gonna stay a little longer tonight, until Janie wakes up."

"She won't wake up yet, Joe, trust me, and I don't want to have to worry about you falling asleep on the freeway. So, come on, it's time for you to get going."

"I love you, Anna," he whispers, holding her close. "And, when we've beaten this, we're going to take Janie to England to see Buckingham Palace. Remember how she always said she wanted to see where the Queen lives?"

"I do," Anna smiles, wistfully.

"We'll make it somehow, sweetheart, I swear," he promises.

Joe leaves, but on the way out of the hospital he knocks gently on the door of an office, and waits. Hearing the command to come in, he enters and greets a doctor who is seated at his desk, reading.

"Hello, doc," Joe smiles, wearily. "I thought I find you here, burning the midnight oil, as usual."

"Oh, hello, Joe, come in. Sit down. You look tired."

"Nah, I'm fine, doc."

"Sit down, anyway. How's Anna doing? She needs to get away from the hospital, you know. It's not good for her to be here twenty-four hours a day."

"Have you spoken to her?" Joe asks.

"Just for a moment, this afternoon."

"Doc, I know things aren't looking good, and I've got to ask you straight out, what are Janie's chances?"

The doctor hesitates: "I understand what you and Anna are going through. You know that, don't you? And you know I lost my own child to cancer, and that I won't lie to you; it's not looking good. I was hoping against hope, but the stats are not promising."

Joe purses his lips and takes a deep breath through his nose, to hold back tears.

"How long does she have?"

"We don't know, Joe, we simply don't know; a few more weeks, maybe."

"God in heaven," Joe blurts out, throwing back his head and closing his eyes, "isn't there any hope, any hope at all?"

"There's always hope, Joe. It's important that you believe that."

"Jesus, doc," Joe chokes, swallowing hard.

The doctor sighs and continues, more sternly.

"Look, everyday we learn something new, and one of these days we'll have the answer."

Joe buries his head in his hands, as the doctor continues to comfort him.

"If I didn't believe that, I wouldn't be here. Why, right when you walked in I'd just finished reading a very encouraging article about an experimental drug that they're testing at the Bane-Wessely Institute in Chicago."

"So if we could get her in there, doc," Joe interrupts, "then maybe …"

"Joe, stop. Don't do this to yourself. First of all, what I'm talking about is experimental, and certainly not covered by insurance."

"I know, I know, doc," Joe interjects, "but if we could let them know about Janie. I could get hold of the money somehow. I'd sell my soul to the Devil, for that."

"Joe, stop talking like that."

He stands up, and walks around the desk.

"Come on, I want you to go home now, and get some rest."

"I'm sorry, doc," Joe says, contritely, "I really am."

"That's okay, Joe. Now go home, and get some rest."

"Yeah, you're right, I will. But, doc, would you mind if I took a look at that article?"

"Joe, no offense, but it was not written for the lay-person, and you wouldn't understand a word of it."

"Look, I know, I'm not the brightest guy in the world, but …"

"That's not what I meant, Joe. It was written for specialists, oncologists."

"Yeah, I understand that, doc, I really do, but would you mind if I gave it a try. I'll bring it back tomorrow night when I come in, I promise."

"Alright, Joe," the doctor agrees. "Here," he adds, turning down a page and handing it to him.

"Now, go home and get some rest."

"I will. Oh, and doc, please don't say anything to Anna, not yet. Leave her with a little hope."

"Joe, you know that I …. Oh, alright," he agrees.

Joe starts to leave, but hesitates at the door.

"Goodnight, doc. I wish there was something I could do for you."

"There is," the doctor replies. "Go home, and get some rest."

CHAPTER SEVEN

At the witching hour of midnight, Marty is sitting on the front porch of an elegant old house built in the foothills of the Verdugo Mountain range, in the city of Burbank. Burbank was established by a wealthy east coast dentist of the same name, who came west to follow his dream of becoming a rancher in the virgin territory of California. In 1867, he purchased portions of two ranchos from Don Jose Maria Verdugo, a Mexican national to whom the land had been deeded by the Spanish in 1798. He sold plots to other individuals with the stipulation that they build a house on the land, but assured the city's ultimate and accelerated development by selling the right-of-passage to the Southern Pacific Railroad for the sum of one silver dollar.

Burbank is a thriving community, perhaps best known for supplanting Hollywood as the home of the giant movie studios, and least known for having once been the residence of the first American saint, Mother Francis Xavier Cabrini. Orphaned in Italy at the age of thirteen, Mother Cabrini traveled to America with the Missionary Sisters of the Sacred Heart, where she devoted her life to the salvation of wayward girls, but became better known as the patron saint of immigrants.

Marty is unaware that he is on hallowed ground, as he sits with his arm around his date, Catherine, gazing at a full moon, and lamenting the fact that he has just spent a day's pay on dinner and an evening out with a girl who now seems as coldly indifferent as the moon itself, a girl that would have made Mother Cabrini proud.

"It's hard to believe we've walked up there" Marty muses, trying to make conversation, "and I sortta wish we hadn't."

"Why?" she replies, shifting her body, to dislodge his arm from around her waist.

"Oh, I dunno. I liked it when it was still a mystery, I guess," he replies, leaning forward to politely distance himself. "You know, like love."

"What d'ya mean?"

"I dunno really. I just remember sitting up in a tree when I was a kid, and feeling sortta sorry for myself. Then I noticed a star balanced right on the cusp of a crescent moon, I think it must have been Venus, and it made me feel better, somehow."

"You were probably just a mixed-up kid."

"Yeah, I probably was, but it did make me feel better."

They sit in silence, gazing at the moon and the stars, until Marty springs to his feet.

"Oh, jeeze, I gotta go," he blurts out.

"So, go. Who's stopping you?"

"No, Cat, I mean I gotta go, I gotta use your bathroom."

"Oh, yeah, well that's not gonna happen."

"No, Cat, I swear I do," he says, squirming uncomfortably as she watches.

"Cat, please, I'm serious. I swear to God."

"Alright, but you'll have to use the one in my room, because the one downstairs is being remodeled. And no monkey business; my dad's the police chief, and his bedroom's right next to mine. You understand?"

"Cat, I swear. I swear on my honor. I really do."

"Yeah, and on your honor you'd better be quiet, as well."

She stands, and they tiptoe across the porch to the front door, where she cautions him again:

"Leave your shoes here and, I'm warning you, no monkey business. And you'd better be quiet if you know what's good for you."

Leaving his shoes behind, Marty follows Catherine up the darkened staircase, with his bowels rumbling like distant thunder. She opens the door to her room and turns on the light, while Marty rolls his eyes and fidgets nervously. With her finger to her lips, she nods toward the bathroom and whispers: "It's in there."

Marty scurries into the bathroom, flicks on the light, shuts the door, scoots over to the toilet, drops his pants, and lands on the toilet with a thud and a sigh of relief. He lowers his head, stares at his pants around his ankles, and groans in dismay.

"Oh, man, would you look at that," he laments.

He unrolls bunches of paper, wipes himself, flushes the toilet, steps gingerly out of his pants, and carefully extracts his soiled underwear. Holding them at arm's length, he tip-toes over to the sink and dunks them under the faucet. Then, catching a glimpse of himself in a mirror, he leans closer and berates the image.

"Would you look at what you've done, for God's sake? You oughta be ashamed of yourself," he adds, wagging his finger at the image.

Then, feeling another ominous rumbling in his bowels, he drops his underwear in the sink and scoots back to the toilet where an incredibly loud fart resonates within the porcelain chamber. He raises his head, closes his eyes, and clasps his hands, as though pleading for divine help, and unwinds another wad of toilet paper.

In the bedroom, Catherine suppresses a giggle with her hand and hears the toilet flush again, while in the next room her father awakens with a start and sits bolt upright in bed. He springs out of bed, grabs his service revolver from the nightstand, and stands motionless in the moonlight with the revolver cocked and raised above his shoulder, listening intently. As the water continues to run, Marty flushes the toilet for the third time and returns to the sink, where he rinses and rings out his underwear and stands shaking his head in disgust.

Marty has a habit of talking to himself, feeling that to utter the words also enables him to outer them, which gives him comfort. And, after staring at his underwear for a moment, he looks up and confronts his image again.

"Ya see this, ya putz? That's five bucks down the drain."

The image frowns back at him defiantly, until Marty shrugs.

"Alright, so they were three for ten bucks; it's still money wasted."

Finally, after contemplating the underwear bunched in his hand and glancing at an empty trash can, he turns to an open window, leans out, looks down, and is about to commit them to the deep when a breeze stirs a leafless twig, which seems to chastise him like a skeletal index finger. He stares at the wagging twig and then at the trash can, and with a sigh of resignation drops the underwear in the toilet and flushes it. He stands, mesmerized, as the underwear circles higher and higher in the bowl, as though yearning to return to him. Paralyzed by indecision, he watches as they rise ever nearer, and then overflow the bowl, splat upon the tiled floor, and glide toward his stocking feet. At the last moment, he hops back and yelps, spontaneously.

"Oh, my God! What have I done, now?"

In the next room, the police chief springs into action, dashes out of the bedroom, barking orders at his wife:

"Call the station, Ma! There's a man in Catherine's bathroom! I'll kill the swine!"

Marty hears every word, and freezes, while his mirror-image goads him into action.

"The window! The window! Out the window, you putz! It's your only chance!"

Laying his pants on the ledge, Marty squeezes through the window, but remains clinging to the sill. Too scared to let go, and hoping against hope that he won't be noticed dangling in the moonlight, he closes his eyes and prays silently through clenched teeth:

"Dear Lord, please help me this one time, and I swear I'll never do this again, never, ever."

The police chief charges blindly through the bedroom, ignoring his daughter's frantic explanation, bursts into the bathroom, skids across the slick floor, slams into the window frame, and finds himself face-to-face with Marty. He grabs him by the throat, and stuffs the barrel of the revolver under his nose, growling with pleasure:

"Gotcha, you fat bastard," he gloats, tightening his grip on Marty's throat.

Marty's eyes grow wide in terror, and with a scream still trapped in this throat he emits a tiny squeal, lets go of the windowsill, and plunges into the darkness without his pants. His shirt inflates like a parachute above his round belly until he lands with a thud, feet-first, and appearing suddenly like a giant mushroom in a bed of tulips. He stands, trembling, amazed to be alive, and unhurt. Covering his genitals with one hand and his buttocks with the other, he streaks away across a manicured lawn, grateful to be free, but hounded by the fear of death.

The police chief appears on the front porch in his pajamas, crouches, aims, and fires at the pallid figure streaking through the moonlight. The bullet whistles past Marty's ear, paralyzing him with fright. He falls, face-forward, and lies perfectly still with his eyes squeezed shut, waiting for the coup-de-grace. But, after a few seconds of silence, and still modestly covering his buttocks with one hand, he raises the other in a feeble surrender, just as a squad car with its lights flashing screeches to a halt at the curb, and bathes him in a kaleidoscopic wash of colors.

"God in Heaven help me," he whimpers.

Marty's arrival in the world was not planned, in fact he was conceived in the commercial kitchen of his parent's restaurant, when they were in their early fifties, and had given up hope of being blessed with a child. Therefore, his conception was regarded as a confirmation of their love, a blessing from the Almighty, and Marty was adored, accordingly. However, he was more or less raised by his maternal grandmother, while his parents toiled seven days a week in their family restaurant, cooking, cleaning, and buying fresh produce for their homemade fare. In fifty years, they had never had a single employee; such was their station in life, which they relished with pride. And by the time Marty's grandmother died, he had already graduated from high school and was working to contribute to the nominal budget of the household, but it is to his grandmother that Marty still turns for solace. Each week, he visits the cemetery, lays a bouquet on her headstone, and shares his private thoughts.

"I know, I know," he confesses, "you don't have to say it, I'll say it: I'm a putz, but I'm going to make something of myself, I promise. You'll be proud of me one day. You'll see."

The dialogue would continue for several minutes, with Marty answering what he believes would be his grandmother's questions.

"Oh, they're fine; Pa still sings in the shower, and Ma keeps on cleaning. They'll go on forever. Yeah, I know, Grandma, but let's not think about that. We all have to go sometime, even me, but I've still got things to do. Right? Well, look, I've got to be going. I've got a date tonight, and this one could be the queen-of-my-dreams, but I'll tell you all about it, next week. God bless, Grandma. I think about you almost every day."

As the moon begins to wane, Marty finds himself alone in a jail cell in, swaddled in a dingy white sheet, talking to himself:

"Grandma, I've got trouble, big trouble."

CHAPTER EIGHT

Early the next morning, Danny stops by Joe's house to pick him up, which is at the west end of the valley in the shadow of the Santa Susanna Mountains. They are temporarily employed by the same general contractor, and Danny has been giving Joe a ride to work since Janie was hospitalized. Joe is seated at a kitchen table with the journal and an open medical dictionary. He turns off a reading lamp, glances out of the window, and sees a blood-red glow of sunlight trembling along the ridge of the mountains and about to flow down the mountainside and onto the valley floor, when the doorbell chimes. He hurries to the door, and greets Danny.

"Man, you look beat," Danny says, as he enters.

"I am," Joe agrees. "To tell you the truth, mate, I'm knackered. I didn't get to bed last night."

"You've gotta take better care of yourself," Danny admonishes, "not just for your sake but for Anna and Janie."

"It's not like that, mate," Joe says, his eyes sparkling. "I think I might be onto something."

"What d'ya mean?" Danny asks.

"Well, there's this place in Chicago where they're testing a new drug, and they've had some miraculous results with little ones, like Janie."

"Hey, that's fantastic," Danny exclaims. "When did you find that out?"

"It's in this medical journal that Janie's doctor gave me. It was tough reading for a dope like me, but there's no doubt that the drug works."

"So, is he sending her out there, or what?"

"No, that's the rub. It's private, and wouldn't be covered by our insurance, anyway. But if they'd only let her in, I'd get the money for the drug, somehow."

"So, how can we get her in there?" Danny asks, subdued.

"I dunno. That's what I've been thinking about. I'm gonna make some calls, and talk to her doctor about it later, when I get off work. Maybe we could just buy the drug from them, and Janie's Doc could give it to her. You know what I mean?"

They lapse into silence. Then, Danny's cell phone rings and he answers it. It's Marty calling from outside the jail, explaining his plight, and asking Danny to pick him up and drive him to an impound yard to pick up his van. Danny and Joe leave in a hurry. When they arrive, they see Marty standing at the curb, his head hung in shame, holding up a pair of oversized prison denims. He apologizes for involving them in his public shame, and although he has been released on his own recognizance he admits that he terrified that his aging parents will find out that their only beloved son has spent a night in jail and been charged with public indecency. Joe tries to comfort him, by telling him that even the defense of a property would never justify firing on an unarmed and semi-naked man, whatever the rank of the police officer, while Danny assures him that the charge is insignificant, a mere misdemeanor that is likely to be dismissed at the first hearing. But Marty is inconsolable, and grimaces as though every reference to the event is a brand searing his flesh. And, although adamant about his innocence, he has very little faith in the legal system, and remains convinced that he will be served up like a sacrificial lamb to the police chief, or beggared by the outrageous fees of a corrupt defense attorney in cahoots with the local prosecutor.

CHAPTER NINE

On the following Friday, Danny arranges to meet with Joe and the rest of the team at the pub. Janie has shown a little improvement, and they want to cheer up Joe by treating him to an early dinner and a frosty flagon of ale. But, Marty is conspicuously absent. Sally joins them at their favorite booth to take their orders, and notices Joe for the first time.

"Hello, love, we've missed you around here. But, I hear Janie's doing better."

"Yeah, a little bit," Joe agrees.

"Ah, that's good news, love. Give Anna a hug for me and tell her that we miss seeing her around here, too."

"I will, Sal. Thanks."

"I thought it was a little quiet in this corner," she adds, not seeing Marty. "Where's our resident Casanova?"

"I dunno," Joe says. "Probably looking for love in all the wrong places, but he'll show up. He always does, like a lucky penny."

"Alright, lads, what will it be, then?" she asks, getting back to business.

"Well, let's start with some Boddingtons and some of those Cornish pasties; we're celebrating an unbroken losing streak," Danny grins.

"Maybe you lads should call yourselves The Losers, next year."

"That's not a bad idea, Sal," Devin agrees, "and it does have a nice ring to it."

She finishes taking their order, and leaves.

"Look at it this way" Danny continues, "we're making the other teams happy. Right?"

"That's right. Doesn't hurt to look on the bright side either," Devin adds.

Moments later, Marty struts toward their booth, grinning from ear to ear.

"Gentlemen," he begins, with a cavalier flourish, "you may have wondered why I'm a successful salesman. Well, it's because I'm a smoooth talker," he continues, answering his own question, and dragging out the word "smooth."

"Don't tell me they dropped the bloody charge against you?" Joe grins.

"That's right," Marty confirms. "I'm a free man. And why?" he smiles, "because I'm a real smoooth talker. That's why."

He claps his hands and spins around, in a clumsy imitation of Michael Jackson.

"Congratulations mate," Devin says, enthusiastically.

"Well done, mate," Joes adds.

But Danny has no intention of letting Marty off so easily.

"So, what you're now admitting to," Danny begins, in a mock-judicious tone and leveling the finger of scorn at Marty, "is that you really did assault the police chief's daughter, but that you managed to talk your way out of it. Is that right?"

"Lower you voice, for God's sake," Marty hisses, glancing furtively over his shoulder, and sliding into the booth. "Of course I didn't, you ignorant plumber."

"But, you just said that you talked your way out of it."

"Well, I didn't mean it like that. What I meant is that they probably dropped the charge against me when my lawyer warned them I'd talk circles around them in court."

"Talk circles around em?" Danny snorts. "You couldn't talk your way out of a paper bag."

"Then how come I'm a salesman and you're a plumber, answer me that?" Marty asks, defiantly.

"What the hell has that got to do with anything?" Danny snorts. "But if you really want to know," he continues, "it's because I do things, while you just talk about doing em. What d'ya think about that?"

"I'll tell you what I think," Marty jokes, "I think you're jealous of my hutzpa, that's what I think."

"Oh, yeah, right, whatever that means," Danny says, raising his hands in mock-surrender. "Hell, you've just talked friggin circles around me."

"Hey, seriously, you guys, listen to this," Marty confides, "because you won't believe this one. That bastard lawyer of mine charged me eight-hundred and fifty friggin bucks. Can you believe that? Eight-hundred and fifty friggin bucks, for a couple of phone calls. And that was money I was saving to send my folks on a cruise for their anniversary. Still, it was worth it, I suppose," he sighs. "Hey, talking about smooth talkers and lawyers," he continues, grinning and winking, "old Hans here is onto a good thing. Right, Hans?" he adds, nudging him.

"Der buutiful lawyer? Oh ya."

"Shall I tell them?" Marty continues.

"Oh, shuer," Hans agrees.

"Okay, get this. Hans meets this female lawyer on the Internet, see, and they've been chatting back and forth, about the law, and golf, and stuff like that. And old Hans must be quite the talker, because she turns out to be a blonde bombshell with great big knockers. Right, Hans?"

"Oh, ya," Hans agrees.

"Anyway, and this is the best part, he's booked a swanky room in the Astoria, and he's gonna meet her there tonight, for the first time. Isn't that right, Hans?"

"Oh ya. Dis wery citing fer me," Hans grins.

"You've got that right, you lucky bastard," Marty chuckles.

They continue with friendly banter until Sally returns with their beers. She endures Marty's usual flirtation, while Danny breathes in her essence, and leaves them to their conversation. They raise their glasses in a toast to Joe, Anna, and Janie, and discuss the commonplace events that comprise the fabric of their lives. But Shawn is withdrawn and cannot sustain an interest in the conversation.

"Look, guys, I enjoy your company," he says, "but I can't hang out too long. I didn't want to have to tell you this, but me and Helen are through, and I'm trying to get settled in an apartment with the kids."

"Jesus, Shawn. When did this happen?" Danny asks.

"We've just been growing apart, I guess. You know me. I'm just a working-class guy, and I think she wants something a little better."

"That's bullshit, mate," Devin snaps. "There's nothing better than a working-class bloke, and that's a fact. They're the ones who plant the crops, build the houses, and keep the lights burning."

"Yeah, but you know what I mean," Shawn says.

"No, I don't, mate, and I'm serious. If you're saying that Helen is looking for some bloke with money and a suit and a tie, then I say good riddance to her. I wear a tux and tie every night, and it makes me feel like a bloody penguin. I mean, think about it, what the hell's a tie for anyway? It doesn't make any sense, unless of course you just want to hang yourself. We might just as well go prancing around naked, or wearing nothing but a penis-gourd."

"What's a penis-gourd?" Marty asks, mystified.

"Ah, it's a great big dried-out thing, a seed pod or something. And some of the natives in the jungle wear it on their …. Well, you know, on their roger. You wouldn't believe it; some of them are this big," he adds, indicating a size.

"Well, what do they do that for," Marty asks, still mystified.

"How the hell should I know," Devin grins. "What am I, an anthropologist? But why are you so interested? I thought you were into knockers, not rogers."

"I am. I'm just asking, that's all."

"Hey, Shawn," Devin continues. "I didn't mean to bad-mouth Helen. I haven't been in the best of spirits, lately, and I guess I got a little carried away."

"It doesn't matter, Dev, not now anyway."

"Nah, it was none of my business, mate. I should have kept my mouth shut. I'm under a bit of strain myself, that's all. Laurie's due in fourteen weeks, and we've got no bloody insurance. So, I've been bowing and scraping, and kissing ass every night for tips, and I've only been able to put away a grand in the last five months; seems like every time we get ahead the bloody washing machine, or the car, or something else breaks down. I don't know what the hell we're going to do. But I can't blame anyone but myself."

"You've got that right," Marty admonishes. "And I warned you, didn't I, you dippy Brit? I told you not to get hitched. You should have kept on playing the field, same as me."

"Hey, what can I say? Devin grins. You're right. But then again I don't have your assets, do I?'

"What assets?" Danny asks, perplexed.

"Well, like his sculpted body, his silver tongue, and his natural good looks."

"You don't honestly think he's good-looking, do you?" Danny taunts.

"Look who's talking," Marty chuckles.

"Don't get me wrong, lads," Devin continues, ignoring Danny's question, "I wouldn't have it any other way. Laurie's the light of my life, but five-thousand bucks would certainly make it a little brighter."

"Shit, Dev, you think you've got it bad," Danny says. "The IRS audited me a few months back, and they've been crawling all over my ass ever since. And last week they garnished my bank account and lifted seven-hundred bucks. And it wasn't even my stinking money."

"So, how did it get in your account?" Marty asks.

"Well, it was my money, in a way. I mean, I'd just deposited a start-check that I'd picked up for the material on a new job, and now I don't know how I'm going to start the friggin job let alone finish it."

"Money's a bitch, ain't it?" Marty declares. "Thank God I'm not married. But, you can't make it being single either. I mean, I spend five days a week working my ass off, I live above my parent's garage, darn near rent-free, and I still don't have a pot to piss in."

"That's because you're out chasing skirt every night," Danny admonishes.

"Well, that's beside the point, isn't it? Anyway," he grins, "as I was about to say before this loud-mouthed plumber butted in, money really is a bitch. Take my boss, for instance, he doesn't do a lick of work, and yet he doesn't know what to do with all his dough. He's got a boat, a plane, three ex-wives, a stable of horses, and half a dozen floosies, and he's still rolling in it. And get this; he has this hot-shot accountant telling him that he has to spend more or give it to the government. It's friggin criminal, that's what it is."

"It's friggin luck, that's what it is," Danny quips.

"Bullshit," Marty counters, "it has nothing to do with luck. I bet we could come up with something clever if we really wanted to. In fact, we should all put our heads together and try to come up with some nifty little scheme, like old Hans did. Think about it, two or three-thousand bucks apiece, eh? That would do for starters, wouldn't it?"

"You know, I hate to admit it," Danny declares, "but maybe Marty's right. And lately, I've been thinking about how weird it is the way things work out. I mean, I never wanted to be a stinking plumber. I just happened to get a summer job as a plumber's helper, and now here I am, twelve years later, down in the dirt and laying pipe. I guess that's just the way things work out in life, eh?"

"Yeah," Devin agrees, "way does lead onto way, as a poet once said."

"Lord, if that's true," Marty muses, "I wish I'd started out in Chippendales. Can you imagine that? All those women stuffing bills in my shorts, and trying to cop a feel?"

"From what I've heard about your shorts, lately, mate, copping a feel could be a very dicey move," Devin grins.

"Oh, shit, that's right," Danny groans. "I don't even want to think about it, cos it'll turn me off my food."

"Well, something should, Marty grins. You're getting to be such a lard-ass; you're giving plumbers a worse image."

"Look who's calling the kettle black," Danny declares, glancing around for support.

"You know, Danny's right," Devin muses. "It is weird the way things work out. We think we've got choices, but maybe we don't."

"Of course we do," Shawn interjects. "In fact, all we do have is choices. And sometimes they're tough, but that's what makes us who we are."

"Maybe we're just too friggin dumb," Danny muses.

"Bullshit," Marty exclaims. "We're not dumb, none of us. I bet if we wanted to we could have just as much money as any of those rich bastards. We just haven't put our mind to it, yet. I bet we could even plan the perfect crime if we wanted to; you know, knock over a bank or something--something that would take a lot of planning. You know what I mean? And that would solve all of our problems. Right Dev?"

"Oh, yeah, right, Marty," Devin replies sarcastically, "and we'd all end up in the slammer, staring at our gourds. You and your big ideas," he chuckles.

"Not necessarily," Danny muses.

"That's right," Marty continues. "I mean, you and Cruz are pretty darn smart, and what about those Brits and the great train robbery, eh? They got away with it, didn't they? And no one even got hurt."

"Yeah, I heard about that," Devin agrees, "but it was before my time."

"Yeah, mine too." Marty agrees. "But I read about it in a magazine and, let me tell you, they got away with millions. And I'll tell you something else as well, there are a lot of smart people out there sitting at computers all day and ripping people off."

"Well, that's it, Marty," Devin declares. "You've just made yourself our bloody leader. So turn on your computer and get about three-grand for me and Laurie. In fact, you can even be the baby's godfather, if you want."

"Yeah, and while you're at it, get seven-hundred for me!" Danny says. "Oh, what the hell make it an even grand." he adds.

"Look, I just sell them. I don't even own one," Marty admits.

"You're shitting me," Shawn exclaims. "You're a computer salesman, and you don't even own one?"

"No, honestly, I can't afford one. Besides, I wouldn't own one if I could; they mess with your life."

"What do you mean?" Shawn asks.

"Well, it's like television; some people spend all their time sitting in front of them, when they should be out and about, and living their life."

"What he really means is chasing skirt," Danny grins.

"Yeah, and why not? That's living isn't it? It's human nature. It's essential for the survival of the species."

"Ooh, essential for the survival of the species, is it?" Danny mimics, sarcastically. "You hear that, fellas? Professor Marty chases skirt for the survival of the species. And all this time I thought he was just trying to get laid."

"Well, that too," Marty grins.

"Hey, Marty," Danny continues, "didn't you just tell us that Hans met some buxom blonde on the Internet."

"Yeah. So?"

"Well, that was thanks to a computer wasn't it?"

"You know, that's true," Marty grins. "I hadn't thought about it like that. Forget what I said about computers," he adds. "What do I know?" he asks, rhetorically.

"Alright, guys," Shawn says, standing to leave, "that'll have to do it for me. I'll see you all later. Joe, you take care of yourself, say hello to Anna for me, and call me if there's anything I can do, anything at all."

"I will, thanks, mate. And you keep your chin up, alright? And give the kids a hug for me."

After Shawn leaves, they become more contemplative.

"So, what was that all about?" Devin asks.

"What was what all about?" Danny replies.

"Shawn, dumping on himself like that."

"Well, he knocked up Helen, and never did graduate. He got into construction one summer, same as I did, and before he knew it he was making some serious bank. But the truth is Helen started spending it as fast as he could make it, but she would never let him forget that he'd never finished high school."

"That ain't right," Marty says.

"No, it ain't. Besides, there's more than one way of being smart. You should see the stuff he's built. He can see the way things should fit together, and his hands are smart enough to make it happen."

"I've never thought of it like that," Devin muses, "but that's a nifty idea. I mean, there must be hundreds of ways of being smart, besides using your head. And, when you think about it a seed is being smart when it pushes its way through the soil and turns to follow the sun."

"Well, maybe it's just using its head," Marty chuckles.

"What head, you dim-wit?" Danny taunts. "Hey, Dev," he adds, "where did you learn fancy stuff like that?"

"In school, same as you."

"I never learned anything like that in school."

"Then I guess I got lucky, didn't I?"

"Yeah, I guess you did, because about the only thing that I learned is how to add and subtract, and I've been doing more subtracting than adding, lately. I mean, what are we, cogs in a machine? My life's ticking away, and I haven't learned diddly, except how to lay pipe. And how many girls are there waiting for the right plumber to come along, eh?"

"You're more than a plumber, mate," Devin assures him," you're our captain, our spiritual leader."

"That's kind of you, Dev, and if you and Laurie ever need an honest plumber, you know where to find me," Danny grins. "But let's get back to what old Marty was saying, because I think he might be onto something. I bet if we were really smart, we could pull off some caper like those Brits. I mean not everyone gets caught, do they? Of course, the police want you to believe they do, but they don't. I actually think the police can be pretty dumb sometimes."

Joe fidgets, uncomfortably: "You blokes are nuts, you know that, sitting around talking about stealing other people's money."

"We're not. We're just having an intellectual discussion, that's all," Danny continues.

"Ooh, is that what we're doing," Marty mocks. "I thought we were just bull-shitting."

"Yeah, we are. But, Joe, look at it like this. They want us to believe that all men are created equal, right? I mean that's what we're taught since we were kids, right?"

"Yeah, so?"

"Well that's bullshit, isn't it? In fact, that's complete, unadulterated bullshit."

"Danny, what are you getting at?" Joe asks.

"Alright, take the Kennedy's for instance, and I've got nothing against them personally you understand, but they sure had a leg up on us at the moment they were born, didn't they? And take that miserable old bastard Getty. Have you seen his friggin museum on top of the Santa Monica Mountains, above the Sepulveda pass? And, do you know that that old miser charged his own son interest on a loan? Can you believe that? And guess what: they're still spending his friggin billions, and he's been dead for years? Died all alone, too. The poor old bastard."

"I thought he had a pretty young wife," Devin says.

"No. He had a mistress. But she wanted him to buy her a house, but he'd only buy her a condo. And that really pissed her off. So, she left him. And he ended up alone, too scared to go to bed, and died sitting up in a chair in his living room."

"Now that's a friggin crime," Marty adds.

"Yeah, so? You can't take it with you? And what are we supposed to do about it anyway? That's capitalism, right? That's the American way, mate."

"Yeah, and I'm not suggesting that we do anything about it, Danny replies. "I'm just saying that there's a fine line between what's right and what's wrong, and between what they want us to believe and the real truth, that's all."

They remain silent, considering Danny's convoluted argument.

"So, Danny," Marty blurts out, "maybe I am dumb, because I'm not sure that I'm following you. What exactly are you trying to tell us?"

"He's a revolutionary, that's what he is," Devin interjects, "and he wants us to overthrow the bloody government."

"You're right", Marty chuckles. "We should never have made him the captain of The Raiders; it went straight to his head."

"Hey, you guys, get serious for a moment," Danny says. "Look, just for the sake of argument, consider this. All of us have got to work for a living, right, we know that. But why is it that some people never have to work? Explain that to me?

"Ooh, ooh, I think I know the answer to that one, Danny," Marty mocks, waving his hand like an excited schoolboy: "Is it because they're lucky bastards, and we're not?"

"You've got that right, Marty," Devin chuckles.

"Funny, very funny, Marty. But seriously, you guys, is it right that money should make money? I mean, money should be tied to material and labor, right? Go on; think about that one for a moment."

"Danny, what the hell are you getting at?" Devin asks, waving Sally over for another round, and holding up his hand to silence Danny.

"Bring us another round, love, but no more for Danny-boy, he's getting a little too philosophical."

"Look, I'm serious, you guys," Danny continues. "Think about it for a moment. If you want to buy something and you don't have the money, you're going to have to borrow it, right?"

"Yeah," they agree in unison.

"Well, the guy who has the money is going to charge you for using it, right? Now, he's not doing any work, is he? He's just got the dough, and that's the only friggin difference."

"Of course it is, you silly sod," Devin chuckles. "If he has the dough, he doesn't have to work, now does he?"

"No, he doesn't, but that doesn't make it right."

"Well, in a way he is working," Devin points out.

"You call that work?" Danny asks, defensively.

"Yeah, I do. Anyway, what do you suggest we do, whack him over the head and take it, or is he just supposed to give it to us?"

"No, of course not," Danny protests, "I'm just pointing out that there's a fine line between right and wrong, that's all. And that sometimes, like old Marty says, some of the laziest bastards in the world end up with most of the friggin dough."

"That's exactly right," Marty chimes in: "the rich get richer and the poor get poorer. That's the way it's always been, and the way it will always be; it says so right in the Bible."

"Well, there has never been any doubt about that," Devin agrees. "Take my boss, Giuseppe. Me and old Cruz worked at his house for his daughter's wedding last year, which is right on the top of a bloody mountain in the Bel Air Estates. It must be ten thousand square feet if it's an inch, and he's got a Rolls-Royce, a Mercedes, two Cadillac's, and a couple of classic cars, but you'd never know it because he squeezes every nickel. And you know what he drives to work?"

"What?" Danny asks.

"An old delivery van, older than Marty's pile of junk."

"Hey, watch your lip," Marty protests, "that's my love machine."

"So he's loaded, eh," Danny grins, "and drives around in a pile of friggin junk?"

"Yeah, he probably doesn't want his customers to know how much money he makes. And take a guess what he rakes in?"

"How much?" Danny asks.

"What d'ya think, Cruz?" Devin asks.

"Between the restaurant and the bar, you mean?" Cruz asks.

"Yeah, approximately."

"I really don't know, but I'd say between thirty and forty thousand a week, easy."

"Whoa. Now that's some serious bank," Danny gasps.

"But at least he's working," Cruz adds.

"You call that working?" Danny snorts.

"Yeah, in a way," Devin interjects. "I mean, he has to sit in his office every night and wait for the dough to come rolling in, and then he has to sort it, and count it, and then stuff it away in an old bag."

"Why does he stuff it in an old bag?" Marty asks, fascinated.

"Christ knows. Maybe he fills his mattress with it, because his wife arrives every Friday night to pick it up; regular as clockwork she is, you could set your watch by her."

"Maybe they don't trust banks," Joe reasons. "My father never did. He kept a wad rolled up in an old sock, at the bottom of a laundry basket."

"No, it's not that," Devin explains. "He's probably hiding it from the IRS; you know, skimming it off the top, like cream."

"Ooh, nice," Danny grins, "and I can't say that I friggin blame him, either."

Joe stands, and drops a bill on the table. "Sorry, guys, I enjoy hanging out with you, but I've got to get back and relieve Anna."

"Hold on, mate," Devin protests. "Put your money away. You've only had one, and you've got another one coming."

"That's alright," he grins, "give mine to Danny-boy. He must be getting thirsty with all that revolutionary talk."

"Put your money away, mate. This one's on me," Devin adds.

"Cheers, Dev," Joe replies.

"Hey, Hans, when are you leaving for Arizona?" Joe asks, as he stands to leave.

"Vun, tuu days, ya."

"Well, you're welcome to stay at my place as long as you want; the door's never locked."

"Ah, ya. Danka, Joe."

"I'll see you guys later," he says, and leaves.

As Joe walks away, they are aware of the burden of sorrow he carries.

"Zo, Joe's leetle gel haz da bad canzer, ya?"

"Yeah," Danny confirms, "and it's looking worse."

"Iz dere nuuthen dey cun duu?"

"No, they've done everything they can. There's some experimental treatment in Chicago that Joe found out about, but it ain't covered by their insurance, and they don't have enough money for it, anyway."

"Maybe ve shuud make da collekshun fer dem, ya? Even da leedle bit vuud help."

"Ya," Danny says, subconsciously mimicking Hans' idiom, "Sally started one about a week ago. In fact, she posted signs everywhere, and is gonna match every dollar that The Roger brings in, but she took them down when she knew we were bringing Joe in for dinner."

Sally returns with their beers, and sets them on the table.

"This round's on me," she winks, "so drink slowly."

She turns to walk away, but hesitates.

"Joe stopped by on the way out, to say cheerio," she confides, "and he's not looking that good, lads, so keep a close eye on him."

"Don't worry, we are," Danny assures her.

Words have the power to nourish and sustain them. But they sit in silence, feeling powerless.

"You know what's strange about money," Devin muses, breaking the awkward silence, "is that most of us don't really understand it, or no one that I've ever met. I mean, there never seems to be enough money to feed everybody and cure horrible diseases like cancer, but there always seems to be enough to fight wars with. And those that have money want us to believe that it's the root of all evil, but it's not. In fact, it's what makes the bloody world go round. And the way I see it, is that the trouble is not with the money but the way in which it's distributed. And isn't that what freedom is all about? It's the difference between wealth, which means well-being, and riches, which means money. I mean, think about it, how much money do the Kennedy's and the Getty's of this world actually need? They eat the same number of meals a day that we do, and they sure as hell can't wear more than one pair of shoes at a time, so why should they have all that dough when so many of us are hurting? And don't expect me to answer that, because I'm not saying that I understand it. I really don't have an answer, and I sure as hell don't have a clue about the way money works, or even what would be best for that matter, and that's a fact. But it really is a mystery to most people, and that's for damn sure."

"Well, shit, Dev, I certainly don't understand it," Marty agrees, "but there's got to be something we can do to get our hands on some dough. You know, I've often thought about robbing a bank," he continues, "not seriously of course, but how it could be done without anyone getting hurt, and no one getting caught. You now what I mean?"

"Christ, that's not what I was getting at, Marty," Devin says, holding his head in mock despair. "Listen to me for a moment, my old son," he adds: "People who rob banks have great big bloody guns, and that's why the people who work in the banks give them the money. Then, Marty, when they've got the money in their hands, they have to run like the wind, which is something that you're not able to do. Now, tell me, Marty, is that what you really have in mind?"

"No, of course not," Marty says, fidgeting uncomfortably. "I don't even like guns, and I'd never hurt anybody. What I'm talking about is doing something real smart, that's all."

"Oh, yeah, like what?"

"I dunno, I haven't thought about it yet. But I'm telling you that I probably could. I'm not as dumb as I look."

"Who said you look dumb?" Devin grins.

"Nobody, it's just a figure of speech," Marty smiles. Anyway, the only figure I'd like to see, right now, is about thirty-thousand bucks that we could divvy up and give some to Joe."

"Hey, that reminds me of a story that I was told as a kid, in England," Devin continues, hoping to lighten the mood. "Apparently, some silly twit went into a bank and, just for a joke, wrote on the back of some deposit slips: 'this is a stick-up; give me all the money,' which the tellers would see when they turned the slips over to date-stamp them. And then, apparently, the twit just stood around and watched until one of the tellers shoved a great big wad of dough in front of some old lady, and she just stood, staring at it, as though it had fallen from heaven and landed right under her nose."

"That sounds like bullshit to me," Danny exclaims.

"Yeah, it probably is," Devin agrees.

"But, you'd have to be really smart though," Marty continues, thinking out loud, "there's no doubt about that."

"I dunno, not necessarily," Danny says, "I mean, how smart would you have to be to grab old Giuseppe's bag?"

"He does have a point there, Marty," Devin acknowledges.

"Yeah, I suppose so," Marty agrees, "but I'm not talking about a simple snatch-job, I'm talking about being real smart, doing something that would take imagination and planning, you know, like the great train robbery, something that would get everybody talking."

They finish their beers and leave. All of them have to be up early for work, including Hans, who intends to rent a pick-up truck and drive to Arizona to collect a motherlode of golf balls, which should fund his vacation and leave him with a small profit.

CHAPTER TEN

Hans has to budget, to make his vacation a success. And, although he celebrates each day, he doesn't waste money on himself. So when looking to rent a pick-up truck he endures a tedious bus ride to a seedy neighborhood in the city of North Hollywood at the east end of the valley, where rental cars are older and cheaper.

The land on which North Hollywood was developed was once inhabited by hunter-gatherers who left no trace of their existence on the landscape, but were rounded up by missionaries and forced to convert to Christianity and live as indentured slaves or be flogged into submission. Their belief in the great earth-mother, and the sacredness of all living things was viewed as quaint and child-like, and never taken seriously as a viable form of human consciousness, a consciousness that saw the world as an indivisible whole rather than as something to be divided, analyzed, and subjugated.

Decades later, most of the valley was sold to large land owners, with the eastern half going to Isaac Lankershim and his friend Isaac Van Nuys, who transformed its grasslands into amber fields of grain. Already wealthy men, they became even wealthier and their names have lived on in the asphalt of boulevards.

In the modern era, the city adopted the name of North Hollywood from its more famous sister city to the south. Both cities have lost their glamour and their fame, in spite of the fact that North Hollywood was actually the cradle of California's statehood.

After walking down Lankershim Boulevard for about twenty minutes, Hans arrives at an old red-brick building, with the name Empire Automotive, on which a banner displays a brood of bright yellow chicks, hopping among broken eggshells, and chirping: "Cheep! Cheep! Cheep!"

Hans enters and encounters the owner, a smiling, turbaned, Indian, who greets him traditionally by placing the palms of his hands together and bowing his head.

"Good Morning to you, sir," he says, with a heavy British accent, "and how may we be of service?"

Surprised by the unfamiliar greeting, Hans stops, and imitates the gesture.

"Oh, ya, guut morning tuu yuu. Dis day I duu da treep to Arizona fer da merchandize, unt I needz da guut mileage truck, ya."

"Indeed, sir, one moment please, I think we have just the vehicle in stock."

He disappears momentarily and reappears, gesturing for Hans to follow.

"This way, sir, you are fortunate indeed. I have just the vehicle for you," he says, pointing to a little brown pick-up with its hood raised, where a tiny mechanic in traditional but greasy garb labors under the hood.

"There, sir," the owner smiles, "and don't be fooled by a little dirt. She's a veritable jewel."

Hans squints at the truck over the top of his thick glasses, as the manager shouts something in Hindi to the little mechanic, who straightens up and bangs his head on the hood. The manager shouts at him again, and the mechanic reaches up, slams the hood, and stands dutifully to one side, rubbing the lump on his head and smiling.

"Come, sir, let's go inside. By the time we're done with the necessary paperwork, Mohammed will have her washed and ready for your pleasure."

They go back into the office, where the owner seats himself and gestures for Hans to join him at the desk. He fills out the rental agreement with an imitation quill and a penmanship worthy of Thomas Jefferson and the Declaration of Independence. He carefully explains each and every provision in the agreement, while expounding on the virtues of the free-enterprise system, and his success in what he proudly refers to as the new-world. But, he is genuinely interested in Hans.

"I'm having a difficult time placing your accent, sir," he smiles, rubbing his chin thoughtfully. "Would it be German, by any chance?"

"Oh, ya. I speak de German, buut I frum Olland, ya."

"A European gentleman," the manager exclaims, throwing up his hands, in delight. "Just as I thought. I'm a world-traveler myself, and I thought I recognized the distinctive manners of a true gentleman."

Hans pauses, lays down the pen, places his palms together, and acknowledges the compliment with a polite nod:

"Oh, ya? Danka. Unt yuu duu tuu, das fer shuer."

They complete the paperwork, and the owner escorts Hans back out and into the yard, with the deference worthy of a visiting dignitary.

"There you are, sir," he gestures grandly, "your transportation awaits."

Hans bows once more, and slips behind the wheel, but fails to start the little truck.

"Allow me, sir," the owner smiles, assisting Hans out of the cab.

He turns the key, and pumps the gas furiously until the little engine gasps, splutters, and finally explodes into life, enveloping the truck in a cloud of blue smoke. The truck door opens, and the owner emerges from within the cloud like a Genie from a bottle.

"You see, sir," he beams, waving away the smoke, "you just have to be a little firm with her, but once she gets going there's no stopping her."

Hans smiles, bows his head in salutation, and slips behind the wheel.

"Now, I'm warning you, sir," the owner says, smiling, leaning inside the cab, and tapping on a gauge with a manicured fingernail, "she does like to drink a little oil, so do keep a weather-eye on her."

Hans puts the car in gear and inches toward the exit while the owner marches ahead like a drum major at the front of a parade. Near the gate, he steps nimbly to one side, gestures grandly, and stands waving goodbye until only a wispy trail of smoke remains.

Hans turns onto a freeway and heads east, outward bound from Los Angeles, and on his way to Arizona. He has the windows rolled down and the radio turned up high, and is singing along with a Harry Nilsson song from the late sixties: "I'm so tired of getting nowhere, seein my prayers going unanswered, I guess the Lord must be in New York city," not that anyone would understand a single word of his mangled English. But his joy fills the air.

CHAPTER ELEVEN

A few miles away on Ventura Boulevard in Encino, a city named by Spanish conquistadors for the "encinos," or oak trees that grew in abundance, Joe enters a bank. A solitary oak remains in the parking lot, protected by state law and on the actual site of an ancient village where indigenous people first welcomed the Spaniards with offerings of fruit, nuts, and water, and where Joe now waits in the hope of securing a loan that could save his daughter's life. As he waits, he gazes about aimlessly at the uniformly bland furnishings. He has dark circles beneath his eyes and appears to be gaunt and even menacing, but he is not. He is a desperate man, to be sure, but not a dangerous one. Only sentimental men are really dangerous.

"Good Morning, sir," the loan officer says, slipping behind his desk. "How can we help you?"

"I'd like to borrow some money, you know, make a loan."

"A car loan, sir?"

"No, I guess you'd call it a personal loan."

"And, I assume you have accounts with us?"

"Oh, yeah, of course. I've been banking with you guys for about six years now. Ever since I got married, in fact."

"But, we've only been here for a year, sir."

"Yeah, I know that, but I mean with Valley Savings, before you guys took them over."

"Ah, I see," the officer nods, turning to the computer, "and your account number, sir?"

"Oh, yeah, let's have a look," Joe says pulling out his checkbook and reading him the account number, which the loan officer enters into the computer.

"And do you have any other accounts with us, a savings account for instance?"

"No, that's it, I'm afraid we've gone through our savings, which is why we need a loan."

"And what about other assets? Do you own your house?"

"No, no we don't, we're renting, see."

"Cars?"

"Oh, yeah," Joe smiles, relieved to be able to finally affirm something, "it's outside in the parking lot. It's a ninety-two Ford pick-up that's free and clear, and my wife's got a ninety-four Jeep that's almost paid for. Just two payments left, as a matter of fact."

"I see, and how much were you hoping to borrow?"

"Twenty thousand, we need about twenty-thousand."

"Twenty-thousand? Well, I'm afraid that's quite out of the question, sir. You see, you don't have the collateral to secure such a loan."

"You mean the money?"

"Well that, or other assets, equity in a home, for instance."

"Well, if I had that, mate, I wouldn't need to borrow the money, would I?"

"I'm sorry, sir, but that's bank policy."

"Look, I need that money. My little girl's sick, real sick, and she needs it to get well. Isn't there some other type of loan, or someone else I can talk to? You know, like the manager or maybe the vice-president?"

"I'm afraid not, sir."

"Listen, mate, I've been banking here for six bloody years, and in all that time I've never bounced a check, never been late on a payment, nothing. That should count for something, shouldn't it?"

"I'm sorry, sir, but it's completely out of my hands. It's bank policy, you see, and I'm just doing my job. I'm sure you understand," he adds, nervously.

"No, I don't, I really don't, mate. And that's a bloody fact," Joe adds, as he stands to leave.

The loan officer fidgets nervously until Joe walks away, and continues to watch him until he nears the exit where an armored guard is about to enter with a sack of money in one hand and the other resting on a pistol.

"Here, let me get that door for you," Joe says, springing forward to hold the door.

"Thank you, sir. That's kind of you."

"Not at all. Would you like a hand carrying some of that dough?"

"No, I think I can manage," the guard grins. "But thanks anyway."

Joe sits outside the bank in his pick-up with tears trembling in his eyes, feeling completely helpless for the first time in his adult life. He sniffs and brushes away tears, starts the truck, and drives away. He takes several deep breaths, trying to compose himself, and is about to pull into a gas station when he sees a man with his pants half-down crawling on hands and knees across the sidewalk. He parks in the driveway, to shield the man, and leaps out with his heart pounding.

"Jesus Christ," he shouts, "I almost ran you over! You can't crawl around on the bloody sidewalk like that. What's the matter with you? Come on, get up! Get outta here!"

To Joe's astonishment, the man merely stares at him, blankly, rocks back on his haunches, raises his arms as though beseeching him for mercy, and cries soundlessly. Joe is dumbfounded.

"Now hold on, Buddy," he cajoles, "you don't have to do that, I ain't gonna hurt you. Come on now, let me help you up," he adds, reaching for him, but the man recoils and opens his mouth as if to scream, but no sound emerges, and Joe finds himself staring at a halo of matted hair around a pink toothless mouth. He hurries back to his truck, backs up, and drives away, trembling.

"Bloody hell, I can't take much more of this," he mutters.

He has been drawn into a vortex of despair, and spirals ever deeper toward that moment of singularity that is death. Miles away, Danny feels the energy being drawn away and resolves to fight the good fight. He drives to the parking lot behind Giuseppe's restaurant and waits for Devin to arrive, who is surprised to see him but knows that the world is becoming a darker place.

"Hey, Danny," he says, "what's going on?"

"It's about Joe. I'm worried about him. He has been acting weird. You know, desperate. I can see it in his eyes."

"You mean, he might hurt himself?"

"No, nothing like that, but I don't know how to explain it. He's like, well, crazy, like he might go nuts or hold up a liquor store, or something. You know, for Janie."

"Oh, man, you'd better talk to him. He could get himself killed pulling off a stunt like that, and then where would his family be? You'd better talk to him, mate, I'm serious."

"Yeah, I suppose so," Danny agrees, rubbing the nape of his neck.

"Would you do something like that," he asks, looking into Devin's eyes.

"What, talk to him?"

"No, hold-up a liquor store?"

"Are you nuts?"

"Yeah, I suppose so. But we've got to do something, Dev. There has to be a way we can get our hands on some dough for him, and soon. They turned him down cold at the bank, yesterday."

"Oh, Lord, is that right?"

Yeah. Sally's collected close to two grand, which she's gonna match, but even four grand ain't gonna cut it."

"I don't know what to say, mate. Me and Laurie have a few hundred tucked away and I guess we …."

"No, Dev," Danny interrupts, "I'm talking about big money, twenty grand, or more."

"Twenty grand! Holy Cow! How are we gonna come up with that sort of dough?"

The question is an integer of a new pattern of energy that is already beginning to take form.

CHAPTER TWELVE

Hundreds of miles away, in the maintenance yard of a golf course in Scottsdale Arizona, Hans and a groundskeeper have just finished loading boxes of golf balls into the back of the pick-up truck, and stand exchanging crisp one-hundred dollar bills, so new they stick together. It is the biggest and best purchase that Hans has made in his short career as an entrepreneur, and he is full of joy, and drives out of the city and into the desert, singing along with the radio, and a song by Country Joe and the Fish:

"Joy to the world, every boy and girl, joy to the fishes in the deep blue sea, joy to you and me."

He hardly notices night descending, until a bolt of lightening splits the sky and thunder rumbles over the mountaintops. He slows to a stop, gets out of his truck, and walks into the desert, to get a closer look at the large white blossoms of night-blooming cacti called Cereus, or Queen of the Night, which have opened their petals in homage to the moon. He stands staring at the succulent blooms and colored stamen glistening with sweet nectar, which point to the moon and a glittering canopy of stars.

"Gott im Himmel," he smiles, raising his arms in praise.

With his arms spread he starts to spin, slowly at first, and then faster and faster until the stars are whirling around him, and he collapses, giggling as though drunk on nectar. Lying on his back, he watches shooting stars and remembers the first time he saw the dance of the Aurora Borealis in the night sky, on the other side of the world.

His reverence for nature is instinctual and perhaps deeper than he knows, and harks back to a time in which his ancestors lived in Finland at the edge of the marshlands, a place where the world literally fin-ished, and beyond which lay the netherworld; a mysterious place of peat bogs, and dank mists, where goblins and fairies lived, and where wizards listened to the voice of the thunder, divined the future, and became prophets who could call down the rain and cure the sick. Such is the mystery of the subconscious, too deep to discern but patent in dreams. A short time later, and with the intention of driving straight through to Los Angeles, Hans curls up inside his truck, falls asleep, and dreams of flying. He awakens before dawn, and watches as storm clouds gather and lightening flickers across a dappled sky of purple and gold.

"Mine Gott, diz Merica shuer iz buutivul," he mutters.

Feeling the same electrical energy of the approaching storm on his skin that the ancients knew well, he jumps into the pick-up and drives, perhaps aided by a force known only to the nervous system of migratory birds, butterflies, and even mammals that allows them to retrace their pathways along invisible meridians. Within a few minutes, solitary raindrops splat upon the windshield but are quickly obliterated by a deluge. Partially blinded by the downpour, and startled by intermittent flashes of lightening, Hans drives on cautiously, leaning on the wheel and staring straight ahead. The storm stops as mysteriously as it had started, and he increases speed until he is streaking through the white heat of the desert, stopping only for gas, oil, and water. Weary, and many hours later, he arrives in the maintenance yard of the Riviera Country Club in the Pacific Palisades, where he crams seven more boxes of golf balls into the passenger side of the cab, counts out the last remaining crisp banknotes, and heads back to the San Fernando Valley through a winding canyon.

Keeping close to the curb, he waves sleek cars around him as his dirty brown pick-up labors through the elegant suburbs of the Palisades. Then, just short of the top, he notices that he is being pulled over by a motorcycle cop. The cop comes to a halt several yards behind the truck, and remains astride his bike, shaking his head, and watching wisps of blue smoke curling from the tailpipe and mingling with the steam from the waterlogged boxes. Hans continues to watch in the rearview mirror, and sees him step off the motorcycle, loosen his chin strap, release the clasp on his holster, and swagger toward the pick-up with his hand on his gun.

"I'm gonna need to see your license, current registration, and proof of insurance," the cop drawls, mechanically. After which he feigns a cough, and waves away an imaginary cloud of smoke.

"And turn that goddamned thing off, before I choke to death," he growls.

"Oh, ya, daz for shuer," Hans smiles, switching off the engine, and handing him an international driver's license and the car rental agreement.

"I'm driving guut, ya?" he asks.

The cop ignores the question, straightens up, stares at the picture on the license, then at Hans, and shows him the license.

"Is this supposed to be you?" he asks, showing him the picture of a younger Hans.

"Oh, ya, daz me," Hans assures him, removing his glasses, and smiling, in his best imitation of the picture. The cop grunts, and shakes his head in disdain.

"And what brings a foreigner like you into this neighborhood?"

"Me? I juust drivin truu, ya."

"Is that right?"

"Ya, daz right."

"You still haven't explained what you're doing in this neighborhood."

"Juust drivin truu, ya," Hans repeats.

"And what's in the boxes?"

"Ah, daz zum golf balls, ya."

The cop leans closer to the window: "Well, in that case, he says, intending to mock Hans' accent, "yuu wuuddn't mind if I tuuk a luuk, wuud ya?"

"Oh, shuer, daz guut," Hans consents.

As the cop saunters to the back of the truck, Hans gets out of the truck, stretches, and groans with pleasure. Startled, the cop turns, draws, and levels the gun on Hans in a single motion.

"Don't chuut, pleeze!" Hans yelps, throwing up his hands.

"What the hell d'ya think ya doin?" the cop growls. "Get over there against that wall, and stay there until I tell ya to move."

"Oh, ya, don yuu vurry! I stand dere, daz for shuer," Hans promises.

"Goddamned foreigners," The cop mumbles, holstering his gun and glowering at Hans, who remains with his hands raised, nodding and smiling. The cop continues to glower, and then saunters to the back of the truck, where he stands, sniffing.

He lowers the tailgate, and releases a trickle of dirty-brown fluid that splashes onto his gleaming black boots. He squints angrily at his boots and then at Hans, who continues to nod and smile at him, oblivious to what has happened. The cop grits his teeth and takes several deep breaths through his nose, in an attempt to control his anger. But he continues to fume, and after staring at the soggy and bulging boxes for a moment, he clenches his teeth, reaches in and grabs one. It falls apart in his hand, and unleashes a chain-reaction of bursting boxes that release a cascade of golf balls.

Startled, the cop leaps back and appears to be tap-dancing on the golf balls, until his feet fly from under him and he collapses in a heap. Hans stands with his hands raised and stares, as his motherlode of golf balls flows down the canyon, bouncing up curbs, rolling over lawns, and disappearing under bushes in the gathering dusk. The cop staggers to his feet, adjusts his gun belt, and glares at Hans, whose eyes are riveted on the ebbing tide of golf balls.

"Mine Gott, dere goes de muney," he mutters, allowing his hands to drop.

CHAPTER THIRTEEN

On the following day, most of The Raiders with the exception of Joe are crowded into Marty's van and on their way to a soccer game. Despair has strengthened their bond.

"So, when's Hans coming back?" Shawn asks Danny.

"I dunno. He spent one night at Joe's place, and then left for Arizona. But he did say that if he got back in time he'd meet us at The Roger."

"How did he do with that blonde lawyer, then?"

"Don't ask. Apparently, it was a friggin disaster."

"Why, what happened?" Shawn asks.

"It's none of my business," Danny adds, "Besides, he told Joe and not me, and I should have kept my mouth shut. But it managed to make Joe smile; the first time I've seen him smile in weeks," he adds, chuckling at the memory.

"Oh, come on, Danny," Marty pleads, "tell us about it."

"No, no way. He can tell you, if he wants to. It's none of my business."

"Oh, come on, don't be like that," Marty whines. "I tell you guys about my dates."

"Yeah, and we wish you wouldn't, mate," Devin grins. "It turns us off our scoff."

"Funny, very funny. Come on, Danny, you know old Hans wouldn't care."

"Alright, alright," Danny agrees, "but don't say anything when you see him. Let him tell you about it if he wants to, okay?"

"I swear. You have my word as a gentleman."

"I thought you were a ladies man."

"Yeah, that too," Marty grins."

"In that case, Danny, you'll have to tell him," Devin chuckles, "that's a sacred oath, for Marty."

"Yeah, I suppose so. Well, anyway," Danny begins, "she was supposed to meet old Hans in the lobby of this swanky hotel, but she walked right on by without even noticing him. Apparently, she was looking for a six-foot Nordic blonde, which is how he'd described himself on the Internet, so she was a little disappointed with the real Hans, if you know what I mean. Anyway, the truth is, she was a little heavy and not exactly the blonde beauty he'd expected either, so I guess they decided that looks aren't everything and headed for a five-star restaurant in the hotel, which set old Hans back another big one. Anyway, they had dinner and a few drinks, and got a little cuddly, I suppose, and then headed up to the room, where she locks herself in the bathroom for ten minutes, while he waits in the bed and watches tele. Then, when she finally comes out and slips between the sheets, the phone rings. So old Hans answers it, and it's some guy asking for her. So he hands her the phone, and she talks for a few seconds, and then tells him that it's her husband, and asks him to wait outside on the balcony until she's finished talking to him."

"You're putting us on, right?" Marty interrupts."

"No, it's God's truth, I swear," Danny says, raising his hand, solemnly.

"She must be nuts," Marty mutters.

"Well, naturally, old Hans had no idea she was married," he continues, "and it turned him right off. But, anyway, he goes out onto the balcony in his underwear, and sits there watching the lights, and planning on telling her to take a hike when he gets back inside. And he waits, and he waits, and when he finally tries to get back in the room, he discovers that she's locked the friggin door. So he pounded on it for awhile, but she'd already taken off. So poor old Hans hunkers down in his shorts, and spends the rest of the night beneath the stars, freezing his Nordic nuts off."

"So how'd he get back in?" Devin asks.

"I dunno. I guess the maid must have let him in, in the morning."

"I can see that I'm going to have to teach old Hans a thing or two about women," Marty declares.

"Oh, yeah, right, Marty, you're the expert, I suppose," Danny grins, intending to mock Marty.

"Lesson number one: whatever you do, don't go out with the police chief's daughter. And, if you do, take a spare pair of shorts with you."

"Well, I wouldn't have blown a few hundred bucks on a dinner and a room in some swanky hotel. That's for damn sure," Marty argues.

"So, he's not a tight-wad is he? Besides, you don't even have a few hundred bucks," Danny counters.

"Well that's beside the point, isn't it?"

"It's precisely the point." Danny counters: "Christ, what I wouldn't do for a few hundred big ones, right now."

"Money isn't everything, you know, Danny."

"I know that," Danny agrees. "Anyway, it ain't what you've got; it's how you use it."

"Ain't that the truth," Devin agrees. "And as much as we joke around, we really do have to stop pissing and moaning and get our act together."

"Hey, you guys," Shawn interrupts, "everyone's got their pride, right? So let's not say another word about this, unless old Hans wants to talk about it."

"You've got that right, Shawn, and we're done talking about it, right now. Hey, Marty," he interjects, "pull into Taco-Rico. All that friggin talk about a fancy dinner has made me hungry."

"Oh, come on, Danny, I'm trying to stick to a diet."

"What, you on a friggin diet? I don't believe it."

"Yeah, me. What's wrong with that? When I'm finished sculpting this body, women are gonna beg for it."

"Beg for it?" Danny snorts. "That's possible I suppose, if they want a ride on a rhino."

"Me? What about you?" Marty asks.

"You just don't get it, do you, Marty? It's not about the flesh, it's about personality and the intellect, neither of which you possess. So, sculpt away all you want."

Marty is about to protest, when Danny spots the entrance to Taco-Rico.

"There!" he exclaims, pointing. "Pull in! Pull in!"

Marty pulls into the drive-thru, and stops beside a six-foot replica of a colorful sombrero with a built-in speaker.

"Alright, Danny, what d'ya want?" Marty asks.

"Let's see," Danny says, patting his belly lovingly: "I'll have three breakfast burritos, a side order of fries, and a large Coke."

"What a lard-ass," Marty chuckles. "What about you guys, do you want anything?"

They decline. The speaker on the sombrero crackles, and they hear a female voice with a heavy Spanish accent say something completely unintelligible. Marty chuckles, and turns to the others.

"What did she say?"

"Don't ask me, mate, I haven't a clue," Devin says.

"Hey, Cruz, you speak the lingo; what did she say?"

"Don't ask me either. That was English."

"It was?" Marty chuckles.

"Hey Marty," Danny interjects, "maybe she wants to see your sculpted body."

They continue to chuckle, until the speaker crackles with another garbled message.

"I can't understand a word you're saying, darling," Marty shouts at the speaker, "but if you can understand me, I'd like to have three breakfast burritos, a side order of fries, and a big Coke!"

There is another garbled response, which Marty ignores and pulls forward to a blacked-out window and waits. Danny hands Marty a ten-dollar bill, as a speaker above the window crackles again, and they hear a similar voice with an equally thick accent.

"Jew ave a beeg cock?"

They burst into laughter.

"Did you guys hear that?" Marty chuckles. "What shall I tell her?"

The speaker crackles again, and they hear the same question.

"Cuse me. Jew ave a beeg cock?"

They howl with laughter.

"Hey, Marty," Shawn chuckles, why don't you hang it out the window, and let her be the judge."

"Yes, I do, sweetheart," Marty gasps through his laughter.

They're still laughing, when the speaker crackles again, and a chubby hand with black fingernails appears, and they hear a voice from the speaker: "Nine-seventy-tree, plis."

Seconds later, Marty is handed the change, a bag of burritos, and a big Coke, and they drive off, wiping away tears of laughter.

CHAPTER FOURTEEN

The Raiders are engaged in another humorous loss, this time in the city of San Fernando, which nestles in the foothills at the base of the San Gabriel Mountains, at the northeast end of the valley. San Fernando became the first city in the valley after Spanish missionaries built a church and mission there in the late 1700's, which they named in honor of a Spanish king and saint. The missionaries immediately cultivated the land surrounding it, which provided food for many of the surrounding villages, or pueblos, but which also led to the ultimate enslavement of the native population, and also paved the way for territorial wars.

After years of secularization and neglect, the church itself was desecrated by vandals looking for gold. Nuggets were rumored to have been found clinging to the roots of onions, and then buried by greedy priests beneath the floor of the church. The rumor was probably unfounded, but not improbable. Nevertheless, the floorboards were removed from the church, after which the roof tiles were systematically looted from it and the remaining buildings, and the mission and its holdings fell into disrepair. After being used as a pig farm for a while, its mud and straw bricks slowly returned to the earth from whence they came.

The mission has since been restored, although the ghosts of priests are still rumored to roam the cultivated grounds, including that of a priest who was said to have been quite mad, and to have danced naked in the moonlight among the grape vines, like an intoxicated bacchanal. But, perhaps he was simply closer in spirit to the earth than to heaven, or believed that paradise was indeed real, and here on earth, which is certainly an intoxicating idea. Today, the mission is a celebrated tourist attraction. But the land remains divided or, in a much older and more meaningful sense of the word, widowed.

The population of the city enjoys strong cultural ties with Mexico and only linguistic ties to Spain. And although its residents are commonly referred to as being Mexican-American rather than Hispanic, a small segment of the populace rejects any such heritage, and insists instead on being called Chicanos. Regardless, if population is power, the Mexicans will rule California once more. But whatever the political and cultural preference of the populace, they take the ritual combat of soccer very seriously, and a crowd has gathered to witness the bloodless defeat of The Raiders.

With a few minutes left in the game, Devin dribbles the ball through the mid-field and passes it out to Cruz, on the wing. Marty struggles to keep up with him as Cruz dribbles the ball past two defenders, and lobs it skillfully across the face of the goal, where Devin has a perfect opportunity to head it into the net. But, as he dashes forward and times his leap into the air, Marty runs blindly into him and bowls him over. Then, as Marty stands trying to recover his senses the ball bounces innocently off his head and over the crossbar. Cruz drops to his knees, and prays in mock anguish.

"You clumsy bastard, Marty," Devin chuckles, getting to his feet.

"What are you talking about? I almost had it, didn't I?" Marty stammers, rubbing his head.

They straggle off the field, exhausted, but happy.

"Well, Boys," Devin announces, "our unblemished record remains: a perfect six straight losses. By the way, what was the final score, was it twelve or thirteen-zip?"

"Thirteen," Cruz confirms, "but we're getting better, don't you think? Marty managed to keep his hands off the ball. At least he realizes that he's supposed to kick it, and not grab it and run. Right Marty?"

"Course I have," Marty grins, good-naturedly. "I'm not as dumb as I look."

"Yeah, and what about his brilliant header at the end?" Devin chuckles.

"Hey, I never said I was a soccer player, did I?" Marty says. "But, talking about players, did you guys get a look at that sweetheart on the sidelines?"

"You'd better watch it, Marty; she was sporting a big diamond ring," Devin cautions him.

"I don't care what she was sporting. Didn't you see the way she kept checking me out?"

"Checking you out," Danny scoffs. "Are you serious? She was probably trying to see her man, but your dough-boy body kept getting in the way."

"My body," Marty retorts. "Have you looked in the mirror lately? You've got an ass like a hippo!"

"I'm not that vain," Danny replies.

"Well, you should be. It's guys like you that have given plumbers such a rotten image. Anyway, you guys can joke all you want, but you won't recognize this body in a few more weeks. Here, take a look at this already," he says, sucking in his belly and lifting his shirt.

"Alright, Marty, that's enough," Danny taunts. "It still jiggles like jelly, but you can relax now and start breathing again."

Forty minutes later, Danny, Devin, Marty, and Cruz stroll into the pub and head for their favorite booth. The pungent aroma of coffee and freshly baked bread greets their senses, and for a few moments allows them to forget their troubles. Shawn had excused himself to be with his children, but is actually ashamed to show the pain of his wife's betrayal, and has gone to ground like a wounded animal to lick his wounds. Joe has taken a leave of absence from work, and is sinking deeper and deeper into despair, and his despair is affecting all of them like a disease.

No sooner are they settled in their booth when they see Hans approaching, and welcome his positive energy.

"Hey, Hans, my old buddy," Danny greets him, warmly, "so how did it go?"

"Nat zo guut diz time," he admits."

"Don't say that, mate," Devin laments. "We need some good news around here."

"We sure do," Danny agrees. "So, what the hell happened?"

"Ah, don yuu vurry nun; iz nat zo portent."

He pushes a money-order across the table, and sits down.

"Luuk," he says, "I gat diz fer Joe's leetle gel, ya. But I vant yuu don geeve it to eem till I fly avay."

"Five-hundred bucks! Jesus, that's a lot of money, Hans," Danny says, turning the money order for the rest to see.

"I vish I cuud geeve eem more, but I don't ave no more to geeve, dis time."

"Hans, are you sure?" Danny asks. "That's a helluva lot of money."

"Daz okay," Hans says, "back ome, I tink of da frenz in Merica vid da leetle gel. Iz guut fer me, ya?" he adds, smiling.

"I know he won't want to take your money, Hans, but the poor bastard is desperate. Janie has taken a turn for the worse, and about the only hope left is an experimental treatment in Chicago, and his insurance won't cover it."

"Do we know what it would cost?" Marty asks.

"I'm not positive, but about twenty-grand, I think."

"My God," Marty exclaims.

"You know, that seems like a lot of money," Cruz reasons, "but it's only a thousand bucks from twenty people."

"Yeah, but there's only five of us, and none of us has a thousand bucks."

"That's true. But what I meant," he adds, "is that we could probably come up with it if we gave it our all."

"Yeah, we probably could," Devin agrees, "but we're running out of time, mate."

"Jesus!" Marty exclaims. "This is wrong. The government should be made to do something about shit like this."

"Don't be daft, Marty," Devin replies. "This has nothing to do with the bloody government; it's the insurance companies. Why d'ya think their names are on the top of skyscrapers, eh? It's because they've got most of the dough. And they got it by not paying for the big stuff."

"You're right," Marty exclaims. "And that's why we buy insurance, for the big stuff, but they don't tell us it ain't covered, do they?" he asks, defiantly.

"So what? There's nothing we can do about it anyway."

"There is, actually," Marty says, "but we'd have to rob a bank."

"You know, there might be a way," Devin muses, "but you lads would have to help me."

"What are you talking about?" Cruz asks.

"Giuseppe," Devin replies, winking.

"You must be loco," Cruz says, shaking his head.

"It could be done, and no one would get hurt. And it would be just a drop in the bucket for old Giuseppe."

"You're loco, man," Cruz persists.

"What's he talking about?" Marty asks.

"Giuseppe, the guy we work for. We told you, he stashes cash in an old bag, and every Friday night his wife stops by to pick it up."

"Oh, yeah, that's what you guys were saying," Marty nods.

"That's right." Devin interjects, "And if you lads kept a look-out for me, I could grab it and make a dash for it."

"For Christ's sake, Dev," Cruz says, "she'd spot you in a heartbeat."

"Not if I was wearing a ski-mask, or something."

"Are you kidding? She knows you, Dev. She'd recognize you, with or without a mask."

"Hey, you two," Danny cautions, "keep it down a bit, would you?"

"What's the matter with you, Dev?" Cruz continues. "Are you looking for, a free ticket back to England?"

"Free ticket back to England, my ass," Danny snorts. "That ain't the way it works, Cruz. The cops would lock him up, and throw away the friggin key."

"All I'm saying is …" Devin insists.

"Don't listen to him; he's crazy," Cruz interrupts.

"I'm not. And it could be done, I'm telling you. But I couldn't do it alone."

"So what do you have in mind?" Cruz asks, rhetorically. "I suppose you're gonna call in sick on Friday, and then rob old Carlotta in the parking lot, and no one's ever gonna suspect that it was you. Is that what you have in mind?"

"Would you two keep your voices down?" Danny hisses, but they're too engrossed in the argument to hear.

"Listen, I haven't worked it out yet, alright. All I'm saying is that it could be done, and Janie would have a chance, at least."

They look at each other, silenced by an awful truth.

Hans has been listening carefully, and just when their silence signifies defeat he offers them hope.

"I vud do dis, ya, but nat urt de aul lady."

They exchange surprised glances, and nod quietly.

"Ooh, shit, you know that's not such a bad idea," Danny murmurs. "Think about it for a moment. No one knows old Hans, and he could be out of here on a plane, the next day."

"The same friggin day," Marty points out, "if there's a flight."

"Now that's something that really could work," Devin muses.

"Ya, I vud duu dis fer da Janie," Hans repeats, with more conviction.

"Holy mackerel," Cruz laments, "You guys are seriously considering this, aren't you?"

No one responds and they remain silent, until Danny leans across the table and whispers:

"Alright, listen. We don't have to make a decision right now; so let's just consider it for a minute. What have we got to lose? Nothing, right?"

"Nothing to lose?" Cruz snorts.

"Hold on, Cruz," Danny says. "I mean we've got nothing to lose by considering it. So, Dev, tell us once again. What happens?"

"It's a bloody ritual, see. Every Friday night around ten o'clock Giuseppe's wife, Carlotta, shows up. She visits with him for a while, and then goes up front to have a look around and say hello to the staff and the regulars. Then, she goes back into his office. He opens this great big bloody safe, and gives her the bag. Then she gives him a peck on the cheek, and away she goes. She's been doing the same thing for years."

"And what you're saying," Danny concludes, "is that someone could just snatch the friggin bag in the parking lot and take off. Right?"

"That's right, and no rough-stuff, just grab the bloody bag, and run like hell. It would be over in a few seconds. And if we all kept our mouths shut, no one would ever know."

"Like stealing candy from a baby," Marty grins.

"What else, Dev?" Danny asks, holding up his hand to stop Marty's levity.

"I don't know. Someone could be waiting in a get-away car in the alley, I suppose, and we could all meet-up later at Marty's place, or anywhere else for that matter. And we don't even have to do that. I'm telling you, it could work. She couldn't run more than a few steps, and chances are she wouldn't even try."

"What about the safe? Could anyone get to that, after hours?" Danny asks.

"Oh, no, that's out of the question," Devin says, shaking his head. "It's as big as a bloody bus, and locked up tighter than a drum."

"Well guys, what do you think?" Danny asks, glancing around the table.

They fidget nervously, looking at Devin.

"What are you looking at me for," he asks, defiantly, "we're just about the only hope that Janie's got."

"Yeah, and the truth is I don't think we have much time left," Danny adds.

"If that's the case, I say we do it," Marty exclaims.

"Well, what do you say, Cruz?" Danny asks.

"I dunno. We're talking about robbery, and that doesn't seem right, but it doesn't seem wrong either. So, I guess I'm with you."

"Alright, Dev, do you want to plan it, or do you want me to?" Danny asks.

"No, in case you haven't noticed, planning isn't exactly my strong point. Besides, you're our bloomin captain."

"Is that alright with the rest of you?" Danny asks.

As soon as they nod in agreement, he leans across the table and whispers:

"Alright, first things first. Right here, right now, we're going to swear each other to silence. Agreed?"

They exchange glances, smile, and nod in agreement.

"Hans, are you sure you're willing to snatch the bag?" he continues.

"Oh, ya, iz no problem fer me. I vud do diz fer der Janie. Yuu tell me vat tuu duu, unt I duu dis fer yuu," he says.

"Is he speaking English," Danny chuckles, "or am I starting to understand Dutch?"

"Alright, seriously you guys, how does this sound for starters?" he adds, pushing the money-order back across the table towards Hans. "Hans takes this, and gets his money back; we can't have anything linking him to Joe. Then, on Friday, Devin and Cruz will go to work as usual. Hans will meet us near Giuseppe's place in a rental car. Then one of us, maybe Shawn, will wait in the alley with the engine running."

"Hang on a minute Danny," Devin interrupts, "Shawn has kids, and maybe he won't want to be involved."

"So do you, Dev," Danny says, "or almost."

"Oh, yeah, I do, don't I? I hadn't thought about that. Oh well, let's wait and see how he feels."

"Now, as I was saying," he continues, "the rest of us will be waiting in the parking lot in Marty's van. And as soon as Hans is in position and we see old Carlotta coming out with the bag, we'll all pile out, rowdy like, and pretend to be going inside for drinks. And that way, when Hans grabs the bag, we could sortta rush around and run interference, if you know what I mean, dash about, like we're all panicked, and create a little diversion. One of us could even shout that he's got a gun. And that would have everyone ducking and running for cover, while old Hans takes off."

"Hold on, mate," Devin interrupts, "now I'm thinking about it a little more, chances are she'll scream blue-bloody-murder when she gets a gander of old Hans in a ski-mask."

"But that's just it, Dev, Hans won't be wearing a ski-mask, will he? I mean, he can wear a baseball cap if he wants to, but nothing unusual, nothing that would arouse suspicion, if you know what I mean. You see, it doesn't matter if she does see him. She wouldn't know him from Adam, and he's not gonna be around long enough for anyone to identify him. And that's the friggin beauty of it, isn't it?"

"You've got a good point there, Danny-boy," Marty says, grinning.

"You're damn right I do!" Danny acknowledges, proudly.

They exchange smiles and confident glances.

"Jesus!" Marty exclaims. "We could probably pull this off. Wouldn't that be something, eh? One for The Raiders and a night to remember."

"How about that." Danny says. "It's almost as exciting as chasing skirt, eh Marty?"

"Well, I wouldn't go that far," Marty grins.

Danny raises his glass.

"Alright you guys, here's to Janie. May God bless her."

"Yeah, and here's to The Raiders," Marty adds, raising his glass: "May we win one, for a change."

They raise their glasses, and smile gleefully.

Shortly thereafter, Devin returns to the apartment he shares with his wife Laurie, who greets him as he enters.

"Hi Darling," she smiles, "did you have fun?"

"I suppose so. I'm so used to us getting walloped every week that I'd probably lose interest if we won one."

"Was Joe there?" she asks.

"No. We probably won't be seeing him for awhile."

"Oh dear, I can't bear to think about them losing Janie."

"I know, I know."

"I stopped by their place, did a little cleaning and the laundry, and left them a note," Laurie continues, "but they never called back. But, the truth is, I wouldn't know what to say if they did."

"There's nothing to say. They know that we care, and that's what counts."

"How's Sally doing with the collection?"

"I dunno. Alright, I guess."

"Dev, is there something wrong?"

"No, why?"

"You seem sort of distant."

"Oh, I keep thinking about Janie, that's all."

"I know. I keep thinking about her as well, and maybe we could help them a little more. We've saved almost twelve-hundred, now, and I really do think that we could have the baby at home, with a mid-wife. We're doing so well in the classes, and besides we're only five minutes away from an emergency room if anything should go wrong."

"That's sweet of you, love, but I don't want to take any chances."

"Darling, women in China have babies in the fields, and go right back to work afterwards."

"Maybe, but were not in China, and I want to have a doctor close by in case I faint."

"Oh come on, Dev, be serious."

"Yeah, alright, love, but we really don't have to think about it yet."

"But, darling, they must need the money?"

"Well, let's just wait and see. We've still got time."

"Yes, but you said ..."

"Well, what I mean is, we don't have to decide right this minute. We've got time to think about it. Let's just see how much money Sally is able to raise."

CHAPTER FIFTEEN

The following evening, Devin, Marty, Shawn, Cruz, and Hans are gathered around a table in Danny's apartment, studying a crude rendering of the alleyway and parking lot behind Giuseppe's restaurant, drawn on the back of a brown paper bag. Danny is confidently in control.

"Hey, Danny, this map's one thing but shouldn't we all have a look at the real thing?"

It's a bit late for that," Danny grins, turning to the others. "Alright, let's go through this one more time," he says. "First, the most important thing of all; after tonight, none of us will ever mention this again, never, ever, not even to each other. All it would take is for some joker with a loose lip to start talking to someone about it, who would tell someone else, and they'd tell someone else, and before you could say jumping-jack-flash it would be all over the valley, and we'd end up in the friggin slammer playing with our gourds. Ain't that right, Dev?"

"That's right, and that's exactly what would happen," he agrees, "so after tonight mum's the word."

"What's that mean?" Marty asks, perplexed.

"What's what mean?"

"Mum's the word."

"How should I know?"

"Well, you just said it."

"Oh, well, it just means to keep your trap shut."

"Yeah, I know that, but what does it really mean?"

"How the hell should I know? What do I look like, a bloody linguist?"

"Mum's the word," Marty repeats, puzzled.

"Oh, I get it now," he exclaims, suddenly. "Hey, you guys, watch me for a minute. When I say 'mum,' my lips are sealed. See what I mean?" he adds, pressing his lips together, and smiling.

They exchange quizzical glances, and shake their heads, good-naturedly, but Devin is touched by Marty's interest.

"Hey, Marty, here's one you'll appreciate," he says. "You eat cereal every morning, right? Well, we get the word cereal from Ceres, which is the name of the gorgeous goddess of wheat and corn. And she has great big knockers. What d'ya think about that one?" he grins.

"That's wonderful, Dev. One day, when I have kids, I'd like to teach them some neat stuff like that," Marty smiles. "Of course, I wouldn't tell them about the big knockers. But, do you know any more like that?"

"Yeah, how about this one," Devin replies. "If you could hold the word 'disaster,' and bend it, it would break between 'dis' and 'aster,' right? Well, 'dis' means 'bad," and 'aster' means 'stars.' And that lets us know that the ancients believed in the influence of the stars."

"Bad stars," Marty muses, smiling. "That's nifty."

"Alright, alright, knock it off, you two. We'd better get on with this," Danny urges.

"Hold on, Danny-boy," I was just getting educated, wasn't I?" Marty grins.

"Yeah, maybe," Danny agrees, "but right now we've got important work to do."

"Hold on a minute," Shawn says, raising his hand, "there's something I'd like to say before we go on.

Most guys will tell a woman just about anything to prove that they love her, right? So, we really do have to clam-up. And, Marty, please don't go shooting your mouth off to any of your women."

"Mum's the word," Marty affirms. "In fact, now I come to think about it, the Brits that did the great train robbery were caught because one of them blabbed."

"No, they were working-class blokes, like us," Devin interjects, "and they would've never ratted on each other."

"Well, I don't remember exactly what happened, and they probably didn't rat on each other, but how else would we even know about it unless some dope shot his mouth off? So, we'd all better keep quiet."

"That's right," Danny declares, taking charge again, "and that goes for every friggin one of us. Now, let's go over this once more. Dev, Cruz, you'll show up for work as usual, and as soon as the coast is clear one of you will turn off the light outside the back door, so it's nice and dark in the parking lot. In fact, it would be best if you could unscrew the bulb, or even replace it with a dud. Hans, you'll show up in a rental car, park it in the alley somewhere, and wait for Shawn. And, Shawn, you'll get the keys from Hans, and be waiting in the car with the engine running. And as soon as he jumps in, it's pedal to the metal, and you're out of there. And Hans, remember, all you have to do is jump in with the friggin bag, slip down in the seat, and your job's done. Just lie back, and enjoy the ride."

"Don't worry, me and Hans have gone over and over it," Shawn assures him.

"And, Hans," Danny continues, "you'll just have to hang around in the parking lot until you see her arrive. You won't be able to miss her, because she drives a great big silver Rolls. As a matter of fact, I think it's called a

Silver Ghost, or maybe it's a Holy Ghost, but whatever it's called you know what a Rolls look like, eh?"

"Oh, shuer," Hans agrees, as Danny continues.

"Me and Marty will be waiting in his van in the parking lot, and as soon as we see her coming out holding the bag we'll all pile out of the van, laughing and joking, like we're on our way inside for a couple of drinks. Then, it's all up to you, Hans. You'll be walking ahead, so you don't appear to be with us, and you'll just grab the friggin bag and run like hell back to the car, where old Shawn will be waiting with the motor running. Ya?" he asks.

"Ya, Ya, Ya," Hans nods, enthusiastically, and they all burst out laughing with the exception of Marty, who seems annoyed by their laughter.

"Look, hold on," he says, raising his hands. "Instead of going over and over this every stinking night, we should be talking about what we're gonna do if something goes wrong."

"You know, Marty does have a point," Devin agrees. "I mean something could go wrong, couldn't it? And we probably should be talking about what to do if it does."

"Yeah, he does have a point, Danny," Cruz acknowledges.

"Now you're starting to think like winners," Marty proclaims, feeling vindicated.

Danny sighs, and prepares to oppose Marty.

"Marty, what can go wrong besides you tripping over your big feet and falling on your silly face?"

"Hey, come on, I'm being serious. Supposing there are other people around, for instance?"

"So? The more the merrier," Danny declares, shrugging his shoulders.

"What?" Marty asks, perplexed.

"Yeah, that's right, the more the merrier. Look, we're there to create a friggin diversion, right? And the more people there are, the more confusing it will be. I rest my case."

"That is the point, Marty," Shawn reminds him.

"That's right," Danny declares, triumphantly.

"Alright, okay," Marty concedes, "but answer me this, and I don't mean any disrespect to old Hans, cos he's a real mensh, but how would you feel if you bumped into him in a dark alley? I mean, he's not exactly the type that strikes fear into you, is he?"

They glance at Hans, and exchange quizzical glances.

"What are you talking about, you silly twit," Devin interjects. "He's not supposed to strike fear into anyone. That's the whole bloody point, for Christ's sake. He's just an ordinary bloke until the moment he snatches the bag, isn't he?"

There's a murmur of relief.

"He's right, Marty, Cruz says.

"Yeah," Marty agrees, "I forgot about that."

"Jesus, Marty!" Danny exclaims.

"Alright, alright. But what if she hangs onto the bag? What then?"

"Marty, what is it with you tonight?" Danny asks, becoming exasperated. "Come on, out with it. What's on your friggin mind?"

"This!" Marty proclaims, pulling a pistol out of his pocket.

They leap back, startled.

"Jesus Christ!" Danny curses. "Where did you get that friggin thing? Put that away, you crazy bastard, right now! You must be out of your friggin mind!"

"That better not be loaded, Marty," Shawn says.

"Relax, you guys," Marty assures them, "it's just a paint-pistol."

"And what do you intend to do with that," Danny smirks, "fix her makeup?"

Everyone chuckles except Marty, and he is not amused.

"You guys can laugh all you want," he says, still brandishing the pistol, "but I'm telling you that if a big bastard like me shoved this thing under her nose she'd drop the bag like a hot potato. Believe me, I know."

"She's more likely to fill her draws," Danny chuckles, "assuming that you don't do it first."

"Why can't you be serious for a minute? I've been thinking a lot about this, and it isn't a lousy soccer game we're rehearsing, you know."

"He's right," Cruz agrees, "supposing she has a heart attack."

"Crickey," Devin blurts out, "I hadn't thought about that. She's a gentle soul, and I wouldn't want anything to happen to her."

"Hold on, hold on," Danny says, becoming exasperated, "that's enough of the what-ifs. We've got a plan, and were gonna stick to it. Marty put that friggin thing away, and let's get on with it."

"You're right," Devin agrees, "but Marty does have a point, Danny-boy. I mean, something could go wrong couldn't it? And we probably should be thinking about what to do if it does."

"At last," Marty exclaims, "someone with some smarts."

"Bullshit," Danny retorts, "you think I haven't thought about this? Listen, if anything goes wrong that's it. It's all over. Look, we're in this together, right? And what else are we gonna do, let old Hans take the rap? No, we're just gonna cop to it, and throw ourselves on the mercy of the court!"

"Throw ourselves on the mercy of the court?" Devin repeats, quizzically. "A fat lot of good that'll do us."

"Listen, you guys," Danny continues, "you might think I haven't thought this through, but I have. Just ask yourselves? We're not a bunch of common criminals, are we? And what would we be guilty of, eh? Come on you bright-sparks; tell me, what would we be guilty of? Come on, let's hear it?" he persists.

They stand, quietly considering Danny's repeated questions.

"Alright, then let me tell you," he continues. "We'd be guilty of trying to save a life. That's right, trying to save a life. And, are we doing it for ourselves? No, we're doing it for Janie, for Christ's sake. Am I right, or am I wrong?"

"You're absolutely right, mate," Devin replies, "and that's the gospel truth."

"That's right," Cruz agrees, "it's not as if we're doing it for personal gain."

"That's a fact," Shawn agrees.

"Okay," Danny says, with greater authority, "that's it then. Marty, put that friggin paint-gun away.

Devin, take this," he says, handing him the map, "tear it up, and flush it down the toilet. Now, are there any questions?"

They remain silent, until Cruz speaks.

"Well, you guys, I guess we've got nothing to do until Friday night."

"That's right," Danny adds, "and this time the friggin Raiders are gonna win one."

CHAPTER SIXTEEN

Friday night begins a weekend of a celebration inside the restaurants along Ventura Boulevard, a weekend when money overflows the cash registers. But on this night an intense tropical storm called an El Nino, named by Spanish fishermen in the fifteen-hundreds in honor of the Christ child, has left the boulevard almost empty and flowing like a river to the sea. Danny, Marty, and Shawn sit huddled inside Marty's van, silenced by the drumbeat of torrential rain.

"Man, it's pissing down," Danny bellows.

"Yeah, who'd have guessed it would rain?" Marty shouts in reply.

"Rain! It's a goddamn deluge!" Shawn screams.

"Yeah, I can't believe our rotten luck," Marty replies.

"Rotten luck?" Danny bellows. "One of us could have checked the friggin forecast. Oh Jesus!" he screams, suddenly. "Would you look at that!"

"Look at what," Marty shouts back.

"The light, the friggin light!" Danny screams.

"Oh shit," Marty gasps.

They stare at the light, which glows like a harvest moon, larger and brighter than it had ever appeared before, illuminating a million iridescent shafts of rain that strike and flare off the asphalt.

"Didn't I tell them to unscrew the friggin bulb? Didn't I?" Danny screams.

"Well, maybe they couldn't, on account of the rain," Marty reasons.

"That's no excuse," Danny grumbles, as they sit staring sullenly at the light.

"Holy mackerel! Now what are we gonna do?" Danny beseeches, throwing up his hands in despair.

No sooner are the words out of his mouth when the light explodes in a shower of sparks, and all of them recoil in their seats, their eyes bulging as they stare into the darkness.

"Jesus Christ, did you see that, Shawn?" Danny hisses, crossing himself.

"I sure did," Shawn agrees.

"Now, that's what I call an act of God," Marty shouts, gleefully.

They sit waiting for their mission to begin, and perhaps entertaining the notion that a force greater than themselves might be assisting them in their criminal endeavor. After a few minutes, Danny consults his watch and shouts to Shawn.

"Have you seen him yet?"

Shawn rubs condensation from the window and peers out into the darkness:

"No, but I guess it's time I got out and had a look," he replies, pulling up the hood of his Parka.

He jumps out and disappears into the darkness, while they sit with their heads lowered, silenced by the unrelenting drumbeat of the rain on the metal roof of Marty's old van.

"Jesus Christ, what's keeping him?" Danny shouts, to no one in particular.

"Maybe his friggin car broke-down, or maybe he got into an accident," Marty reasons.

"Shit, he'd better show!" Danny growls.

"I warned you guys, didn't I?" Marty shouts. "I repeatedly said ...." But before he can continue, Danny interrupts him.

"Marty, will you shut-up, for Christ's sake? Old Hans won't let us down."

"And what do you intend to do if he does, brave captain?" Marty smirks.

"He won't, I'm telling you."

"Hold on, is that him?" Marty shouts, squinting through the glass at a huddled figure splashing toward them.

"Nah, that's not him. That's just Shawn coming back."

Danny lowers the window to talk with Shawn.

"Hey, Danny," Shawn says, wiping rain from his face, "I can't find old Hans anywhere."

"Shit!" Danny curses, stamping his foot.

"And I'm getting friggin soaked," he adds, "Oh well, what the hell. I guess I'd better keep on looking."

He turns, and runs a few feet away, but turns and runs back.

"What shall I do if he doesn't show?"

"Just keep a lookout for the friggin Rolls," Danny replies, "and dash right back here as soon as you see it."

"But who's gonna grab the bag?"

"I dunno, I dunno," Danny says, flustered. "Let me think about it, for a minute."

"Danny, we don't have time to think about it. We've got to decide, and now."

"Alright, alright, give me a moment. Look, how do you feel about that?"

"Me? I'm not doing it. It wasn't my idea. Besides, I've got kids, and ..."

"Hold on, hold on, you two," Marty interrupts, "I knew something like this might happen, and you don't have to worry, cos I'm gonna take care of everything. All you guys have to do is back my play."

They exchange quizzical glances, and stare at Marty. Shawn sticks his head inside the window.

"Back your play? What the hell is that supposed to mean?"

"Yeah, what's that supposed to mean?" Danny repeats, staring at Marty. "What the hell do you plan on doing, anyway?"

"What do you think I'm gonna do?" Marty shouts, "I'm gonna grab the friggin bag and run like hell, just like we planned."

"Alright," Danny gasps, relieved. "That's the plan, then," he confirms. "If Hans doesn't show, Marty grabs the friggin bag. And, Shawn, you get back out there and keep a look-out for the Rolls, and hustle back here as soon as you see it."

"You've got it," Shawn confirms. "Oh, and thanks, Marty," he adds, nodding at him, "we owe you one."

"Shoot, it's gonna be my pleasure. And we're really gonna shine," Marty grins.

Shawn dashes off through the pouring rain, while the tension builds inside the van.

"Hey, Marty," Danny says, "since I'm gonna be driving this heap, we'd better switch seats."

"Oh, yeah, right," Marty agrees.

As they're switching seats, Marty voices a concern.

"Hey, Danny-boy, what happens if she sees me jump out of the van and then jump right back in again, with the friggin bag?"

"Don't worry, she won't to be able to see a thing in this friggin weather and, anyway, I'll be waiting for you out in the alley, won't I?"

"Oh, yeah, that's right," Marty replies, reassured.

They sit in silence for a few more moments, until Danny notices that the keys are not in the ignition.

"Hey, Marty," he shouts, "if I'm gonna haul your sculpted body out of here, I'm gonna need the friggin keys, aren't I?"

"Ooh, shit, I forgot," Marty says, fumbling in his pocket. "Sorry, Danny-boy."

Danny reaches for the keys, and notices that his hand is trembling.

"Oh, man, we're starting to cock-up," he says, "and we haven't even started yet."

"Hey, relax." Marty says, with feigned bravado, "I told you, I've got it covered. Just keep the engine running, that's all."

The neon sign for Giuseppe's restaurant blinks on and off, high above a rooftop at the end of the block, and six or seven buildings away from the restaurant. Misled by the location of the sign at the end of the block, Hans waits in the shadows outside the wrong building. He is soaking wet and shivering uncontrollably, as he stands with his back to the building with his head down, holding his collar tightly around his neck. From time to time, he wipes his glasses, and dashes to and from the alleyway, looking around frantically for his co-conspirators and failing to understand how so many people could have been swallowed up in the storm.

Inside the van, Danny tries to restore his confidence and leadership.

"Marty, as soon as you jump out," he says, "pull your hood up, and keep your head down. You know, like you're hurrying inside out of the rain."

"I don't have a hood," Marty replies, innocently.

"Oh, shit," Danny sighs. "Oh well, whatever you do, don't let her get a good look at you. Keep your head down and, remember, no rough-stuff, and no yelling; just grab the friggin bag, and run like hell back to the van, and be careful you don't trip and fall on your face."

"Don't worry, I know what I've got to do," Marty assures him, "Believe me, I've been thinking about this, for days."

Marty remains poised, holding the door handle and staring out into the darkness.

"Jesus!" Danny yells all of a sudden, scaring Marty. "She should have been here by now! And where the hell is Shawn?"

"Danny, calm down, for God's sake," Marty shouts, "you scared the shit out of me. I told you not to worry. Everything's under control."

"Alright, alright, but, don't forget, no rough stuff, just grab the friggin bag and run like hell, and for Christ's sake don't trip and fall. And I'll be waiting for you with the engine running."

"Where?"

"What do you mean, where?" Danny squeals, frantically. "In the friggin alley! Where else?"

"Yeah, I know, but which side?"

"It's a one-way alley, for Christ's sake, Marty!" Danny shouts. "Oh, Sweet Jesus," he moans, throwing his hands up in the air.

"Oh yeah, right. Sorry. So, look, keep the engine running. Okay?"

"Oh shit, Marty, maybe we should just call the whole friggin thing off."

"Stop worrying, for God's sake. I know what I'm doing," Marty assures him.

"Jesus Christ, Marty, I hope so."

CHAPTER SEVENTEEN

Darkness creates illusions, but in the torrential rain the area behind Giuseppe's restaurant has been transformed into a squall of dark shapes, looming shadows and isolated patches of reflected light. Shawn sloshes through the parking lot leaving a wake like a little ship, as he searches for Hans. He is cold, and wet, and looks around nervously for a convenient place to relieve himself. Noticing a trash container, intermittently lit by the blinking neon sign of The Magic Carpet Store, he dashes over to it, unzips, and starts to pee.

"Ah, that's better," he sighs, but is startled by a disembodied voice from the darkness.

"Hey, watch out!"

He leaps back, adjusts himself, and stares as a homeless man emerges from behind the trash container, draped in a carpet remnant.

"Oh man! You scared the piss out of me," Shawn gasps, not intending the irony.

"I'm sorry, mister, but I thought you were gonna piss on me."

"Jeez. I'm sorry, man."

"That's okay, mister," the man replies, pulling his carpet-cape around himself, "but if you could spare a little change, I could sure use a cup of coffee."

"Oh sure, man," Shawn says, reaching for his wallet, pulling out a twenty, and handing it to him.

The man stares at the twenty, and looks up in utter disbelief as Shawn pulls two more twenties from his wallet and hands them to him.

"Here, get yourself a room for the night."

As the money exchanges hands, two cars glide unnoticed down the alleyway.

"Thanks mister," the homeless man beams. "Were you a marine, by any chance?"

"No, I was never in the military," Shawn replies.

The homeless man stuffs the money in his pant's pocket, wipes his palm on his carpet-cape, and extends his hand, his eyes sparkling with joy.

"I'd like to thank you, mister," he says.

"No, that's alright, man," Shawn says, ignoring the man's outstretched hand. "I just took a piss."

"Oh yeah, that's right," the man agrees.

Then, he leans forward, confidentially, and looks deep into Shawn's eyes.

"I used to be a Marine, you know," he confides, "Two tours in Vietnam. Got the Purple Heart."

"Did you now?" Shawn answers, blinking, and wiping rain from his face.

"That's right," the man nods, "and I've still got the shrapnel in my head and legs to prove it."

"Well, look, I've got to get going," Shawn says, excusing himself. "I'm looking for buddy of mine, but take care of yourself, try to stay dry, and get out this mess."

Danny and Marty sit silently, and appear to be falling asleep, until headlights illuminate them inside the van and they duck, reflexively. They remain hunched forward and out of sight as a silver Rolls-Royce glides silently through the alley, followed closely by an old red Cadillac with menacing fins.

The Rolls stops and Carlotta struggles out, fumbling to open an umbrella. At the same time a man with a ski-mask over his face and a gun in his hand, steps out of the Cadillac and into a brimming pot hole, twists his ankle, and falls in a heap. By the time he gets to his feet and adjusts his ski-mask so he can see, Carlotta has disappeared inside the restaurant, oblivious to the danger. The masked bandit stamps his foot in disgust, grimaces in pain, and hobbles back inside the Cadillac. Danny and Marty sit up, unaware of the little drama that had just transpired.

Meanwhile, as Shawn continues to search for Hans, Hans is searching for him, squinting through his rain-spotted glasses and seeing only a kaleidoscopic world of iridescent raindrops.

Time passes slowly for those who wait, but for men on a dangerous mission, like Danny and Marty, time seems to be suspended.

"What time is it?" Marty asks, squinting through the window.

"Ten fifteen," Danny replies.

"She should have been here by now, shouldn't she?"

"I dunno. She's probably running late on account of the rain. Maybe she ain't coming."

"I wonder where the hell Shawn is."

"Christ knows. He must still be looking for Hans. But never mind that, you'd better be ready to move."

"What are you talking about? I am ready."

"Whatever. And, remember, no rough-stuff. Just stay calm and, don't forget, act natural. In fact, come on, let's practice," Danny suggests, glancing nervously at Marty.

"Hey, Marty, that sure was a great goal you scored," he begins.

"What goal?" Marty asks, taking him literally.

"We're just pretending, for Christ's sake!"

"Oh yeah, right, I get it. Yeah, that was a great goal wasn't it? And I'll probably score another one tomorrow, maybe even two, if I'm lucky," he adds.

Danny leans forward and rubs the windshield with his sleeve.

"Shit!" he screams. "Isn't that a friggin Rolls?"

"Where?" Marty shouts, straining to see through the glass.

"There! Right there!" Danny screams, pointing.

"Good God, what happened to Shawn?" Marty replies. "He was supposed to warn us."

"Never mind that now. Oh shit, Marty, I think that's her coming out the back door."

They stare, dumfounded, as Carlotta emerges from the restaurant. She is hunched under an umbrella, and doesn't appear to have the bag.

"She doesn't have it," Marty gasps, his forehead resting on the glass.

"I don't believe it," Danny moans, "she doesn't have the friggin bag! Whoa, hold on, yes she does, it's under her arm. See?"

"Oh, shit, she does!" Marty squeals, in delight.

"Marty! Marty!" Danny bellows, bouncing up and down in his seat. "This is it! What the hell are you waiting for? Get out there, and do it!"

Marty flings the door open, and leaps out into darkness. Danny fumbles with the ignition with his eyes glued on Carlotta, and sees the robber jump out of the Cadillac, hobble toward her, and thrust a gun in her face. She raises her hands, reflexively, and the bag drops from under her arm and splashes on the asphalt.

"Oh, Jesus," Danny shrieks, "she's being robbed. Marty, where the hell are you?"

He remains frozen at the wheel, staring at the robber, and mumbling in anguish.

"Marty, where are ya? Oh Jesus, Marty, he's got a friggin gun. Please don't mess with him, Marty. He could kill you."

Danny slips out of the van, pulls off one of his shoes to use as a weapon, crouches down, and circles around the cars, intending to come up behind the robber and bop him on the head. Peering around the back of Giuseppe's old delivery van, he spots Marty tiptoeing toward the masked bandit, who is pointing the pistol at Carlotta while groping blindly for the bag. And he doesn't even notice Marty until he is upon him, and pointing the paint-gun at him in a bad imitation of Dirty Harry. Danny stares, mesmerized by Marty's bravado.

"Hold it right there, partner, and drop that friggin gun," Marty smirks.

The robber is bent over, clutching the bag, but lays his pistol on the asphalt and raises one hand in a cautious surrender. Carlotta remains frozen, with her eyes flicking from Marty to the robber.

"Now, get down on the ground and spread your hands out in front of you," Marty orders.

"But, it's wet," the robber protests.

"You heard me," Marty growls, growing bolder. "You wanna get a little wet, or would you rather be soaked in blood?"

Danny stares, spellbound. And when the robber is spread-eagled on the ground, and Marty is bent and covering him with the paint gun, he leaps out of the shadows, slaps Marty heartily on the back, and shrieks with a mixture of joy and relief.

"Friggin fantastic, Marty!"

Startled, Marty squeezes the trigger and blasts the robber in the wrist with a dollop of red paint. The robber raises his arm, and stares at his wrist in horror.

"You shot me, you fat bastard," he grimaces, staring as a gooey red blob oozes down his arm.

"No, you didn't! It's paint! It's fuckin paint," he squeals, lunging for his gun.

As Marty and the bandit struggle for the gun, Carlotta staggers out of the parking lot and straight into the arms of Hans. She flails at him in a futile attempt to escape, but he grips her by the shoulders, and attempts to calm her.

"Pleeze! Pleeze!" he begs.

But all she can see in the driving rain are beady black eyes behind thick lenses, and the face of her own fear. She closes her eyes to blot out the image, and screams to high heaven:

"Holy Mary, mother of God!"

With mascara running down her rouged face, she appears like a specter out of the Nordic netherworld that had traumatized Hans as a child, and he stares at her spellbound, until she opens her mouth and fills the night with yet another blood-curdling scream.

"Rape!"

"No! No!" Hans protests, "I don duu dis to de aul peeples."

A blurred figure streaks by Hans and into the parking lot. Recognizing it as Shawn, Hans releases Carlotta and chases after him, while Carlotta escapes into the alley. The scene in the parking lot is blurred by the downpour, but similar to the bumbling action of The Raiders on the soccer field. Marty and the robber wrestle for the gun, until Shawn leaps onto the robber's back, which collapses them, and knocks the gun from their grasp. Danny takes a running kick at it but, with a shoe missing, he slips and connects with the money bag instead, which hits Hans in the stomach, and drops him to his knees. They are scrambling to their feet, when Danny takes another running kick, which catches the bandit in the groin and doubles him over long enough for Marty to leap on his back, where he remains perched like a giant bullfrog until Danny leaps on top of him, and the three of them collapse. They fall close enough to the gun for Danny and the bandit to reach it, but Shawn kicks it away. Then Shawn and Hans throw themselves on top of Danny and Marty, and pin the hapless robber beneath a mound of heaving flesh.

Giuseppe appears, silhouetted in the back door of the restaurant, bellowing for Carlotta, and then dashes out into the parking lot. He hesitates at the pile of bodies, but disappears in the darkness, shouting his wife's name. He discovers her leaning against a chain link fence, dazed, and disheveled. Overcome by emotion, he clasps her face, and weeps.

"Momma, Momma. Oh, Momma, you arra safe."

"Sweet Jesus, Poppa," she croaks, shaking her head in despair, "they stole our money, and one of them tried to rape me."

"No, Momma, no. Dey was asaving you!"

"Saving me?" she questions, her eyes widening, in disbelief.

"Dassa right, Momma. An youzza safa now, witha Poppa."

Within seconds, several patrol cars streak into the alley from both ends, with their lights flashing, and block the exit to the parking lot. Two officers leap out, and as one directs a searchlight on the stack of bodies the other levels a shotgun over the hood of the car, as two others advance with pistols at arm's length.

"It's alright gentlemen," Devin shouts. "These lads have got him."

"Yeah, that's right," Cruz adds, "so please be careful with those guns. Everything's under control, and we don't want anyone getting shot."

Somewhat convinced by the authority of men in tuxedoes, the police officers relax, without relinquishing their advantage.

"Don't move, any of you," one officer commands. "Now, who's got the gun?"

"Here it is," Devin exclaims, reaching to pick it up.

"Don't touch it! Kick it toward me," the officer adds, sternly.

"Oh, yeah, right," Devin agrees, kicking it toward him. "And Marty's got one too, but it's only a paint-gun."

"A what-gun?" the officer queries.

"A paint-gun. You know. It shoots paint-pellets."

"Well, whatever it shoots, sir, kick it over here."

"Sorry, officer, but I don't know where it is" Devin explains.

"Here, I've got it," Marty croaks, his voice muffled by a mass of bodies."

His hand appears from beneath the bodies, and flicks the paint gun toward the officer. A second officer approaches, and retrieves both guns. He tucks the paint gun under his arm, and removes bullets from the real one. And as he does, more squad cars streak soundlessly into the alley with their lights flashing, and a swarm of armed officers converge on the parking lot. The staff and a few patrons are crammed inside the back door of the restaurant, watching as the bandit is cuffed and led away, and The Raiders regroup.

"So they collared you with a paint-gun," one officer taunts the robber.

"Yeah, that's right," Marty confirms, smiling, and brushing dirt and water off himself.

"I'll get you for this, you fat bastard," the robber snarls.

"Are you talkin to me? Are you talkin to me?" Marty smirks, in his best imitation of the Dinerro character, which amuses the officers.

The Raiders stand in the rain, too wet to care, and gaze at the colorful spectacle of squad cars and flashing lights in the alleyway, as the robber is placed in a squad car.

"Holy smoke, would you look at that, mate," Devin says to Shawn, who is closest to him, "you'd think there'd been a bloody murder."

"The LAPD doesn't mess around," Shawn assures him.

"I can see that," Devin agrees.

They continue to stare, as a small crowd gathers in the parking lot. But one figure stands out from the rest beaming with delight, and standing with his closed fist raised in triumph, like a wizard who has just called down the rain. His face is wet and shining, and radiant with color.

"Hey, Shawn, what's he so happy about?" Devin asks, nodding toward the figure.

"Him? He's a homeless guy, an ex-marine, who got the Purple Heart in Vietnam."

"How do you know all that?" Devin asks, perplexed.

"It's a long story. I'll tell you later," Shawn promises.

CHAPTER EIGHTEEN

The police disperse a few onlookers, and arrange with Giuseppe to conduct a more formal interrogation inside the restaurant. Regardless, Giuseppe has insisted that everyone come inside out of the rain, for coffee and refreshments. Maurice has rapidly prepared a buffet of hors d'oeuvres and pastries, and sets out carafes of freshly brewed coffee, and graciously welcomes everyone.

The restaurant is warm and inviting, but its romantic ambience has been dispelled by brazen house lights, which illuminate patches of worn carpet and the faded frescoes of Roman Gods and Goddesses. The officers form a colorful throng in their garish yellow rain gear, as they stand around chatting amicably, eating pastries, and sipping coffee, while Giuseppe moves among them extolling the virtues of his restaurant and the culinary talents of its head chef. Meanwhile, Marty is being interviewed alone, while Danny, Devin, Shawn, Hans, and Cruz are being interviewed by a sergeant in a booth on the opposite side of the dining room.

"Alright, let's go over this one more time, if you don't mind," the sergeant says, addressing himself primarily to Danny, "because I want to be sure that I've got it straight. You guys are on the same soccer team, and you three stopped by here to have a drink and say hello to these two," he says, gesturing with his finger. "Is that right?"

"Yeah, that's right," Danny agrees, "but we actually stopped by to talk about another friend of ours. His name's Joe and his kid's real sick with cancer, and we've been trying to get some dough together to help them, but it ain't been easy. If you know what I mean?"

"Yes, I do. Cancer's nasty stuff, and I'm really sorry to hear about that, but we'd better get back to what happened tonight."

"Yeah, right."

"So you guys actually witnessed the suspect assaulting the owner's wife in the parking lot. Is that correct?" he adds, consulting his notebook.

"Yeah, that's correct," Danny confirms.

The sergeant leans back, and smiles.

"And then you say this friend of yours, Marty, jumped out of his van with a paint-pistol and collared the suspect?"

"Yeah, that's right," Danny nods, "and then we all jumped on top of him and held him down, and that's when you guys arrived. I mean, that's when the first officers arrived."

The sergeant closes his notebook, and leans back.

"Well, gentlemen, I think that'll do it. We might have a few more questions later, but I can tell you this much; you guys were lucky, tonight. He had a loaded thirty-eight, with one in the chamber. Not exactly a match for a paint-gun," he adds, raising his eyebrows.

"No shit." Danny agrees.

"Yep, that's right. Well, thanks again for your help. If there were more citizens like you, there'd be a lot less crime; not that we want you putting yourselves in harm's way. That's our job. Now, if you'll excuse me, I'll go over there and thank your buddy, Marty."

"Oh, yeah, go ahead. He'd appreciate that, cos he really respects you guys. So, ugh, that's it then, eh? We're free to go, right?"

"Oh, sure. Sorry to have kept you this late. I know it's been a long day for you guys."

"Yeah, it has. Well, hear that boys? We're free to go. And we do have a game in the morning," he adds, winking, "and then after that we've got to drive Hans to the airport. So let's grab Marty, shall we and be on our merry way?"

"Yeah, why not," Devin agrees.

"And who knows, with a little bit of luck we might even win one," Danny adds.

"I think we already did, mate," Devin adds, winking at him.

The Sergeant isn't paying attention to them, but Danny glares reprovingly at Devin.

"Well, that's enough said, for one night," Danny says, pointedly. "Why don't we get old Marty and piss-off, as you Brits like to say?"

"Yeah, why not," Devin agrees, chuckling.

Giuseppe has been watching the homeless man stuffing one pastry after another into his mouth, and as the group walks across the dining room to join Marty he intercepts Devin, steers him to one side, and nods toward the homeless man.

"Who izza he, anna wherizee come from?" he whispers.

"I haven't a clue, boss," Devin replies.

"Well, izza he onna your team, or what?"

"No, he's not one of ours, boss."

"Wella, fine outta whoa he iz, and getta rid of him, eh, before he hogz alla my pastries. He looksa like a bum, but he mighta be wonna doze undercover boyz, so bea careful howa you talka ta him."

Devin approaches the homeless man, and smiles: "Hey, man, you know Shawn, right?"

"Shawn? Who's Shawn?" the homeless man asks, puffing out tiny clouds of powdered sugar. "Never eard of him."

"Yeah, you have," Devin says taking out his wallet, "and he wanted me to give you some dough, but let's go somewhere private, shall we?"

With Giuseppe watching, Devin steers the homeless man out of the dining room to the back door, with the promise of money.

"Look, Shawn asked me to give you this," he says, handing him two twenties, "but you've got to leave now, and not come back. You understand?"

"Is he a marine?" the homeless man asks, staring at the twenties in disbelief.

"No he's just a nice guy. So, here, take it. But you've got to piss-off, or the police might get mad, if you know what I mean."

"Oh, yeah, I do. I've seen em get mad."

He takes money, and grins. Devin opens the door, and they stand looking out into the pouring rain.

"Were you a marine, then?" the homeless man asks.

"No, sorry, mate, just an ordinary bloke."

"I knew that, cos you're British, aren't you?"

"I am," Devin agrees.

"But you could still be a marine, you know."

"Yeah, I suppose so."

The homeless man smiles, secretively.

"Well, here goes nothing," he says, offering his hand. They shake, and the homeless man turns up his collar, against the weather.

"Semper fi," he grins, but Devin has no idea what he means.

"If you say so, mate. Take care of yourself now, alright?"

Holding his collar, the man leaps out into the pouring rain, renewed.

CHAPTER NINETEEN

The robbery made the local news, not accurate in its details, but entertaining, and delivered like a rehearsal, with the newscaster reading from a script.

"Four local men and a visitor from Finland are being hailed as heroes, after capturing a follow-home bandit who had managed to elude police officers for years. And our own Lucy Alvarez has the story: Lucy."

The camera cuts to a live broadcast from the parking lot of Giuseppe's restaurant, where a female reporter is seen preening herself for a live telecast. The sun is shining, and in the background the homeless man can be seen waving and smiling at the camera, and perhaps reminding some viewers of the biblical axiom that the poor will always be with us.

"Thank you Jerry," she begins. "A few days ago in this very parking lot, Marty Bloom, a twenty-eight year old computer salesman, and four of his companions showed the world that chivalry is not dead. Armed with nothing more than a toy pistol, these men risked their lives to capture a follow-home bandit who had viciously beaten a restaurant owner and his wife, and stolen their meager savings. The men declined our invitation to be interviewed, but we did learn that these remarkable men are not looking for thanks, but are desperately seeking donations from the public that could save the life of a friend's desperately ill child. This is Lucy Alvarez, of Channel Ten News, coming to you, live, from the San Fernando Valley. Back to you, Jerry."

"Remarkable men indeed," the studio newscaster agrees. "So, not only is chivalry alive, Lucy, but common decency and human kindness, as well. And there are those who say that Los Angeles has no soul. Well, Lucy, we certainly thank you for that one."

The newscaster rearranges his script, and turns to face another camera.

"In other news, a man was arrested today after dropping his trousers and bending over in front of the White House, to protest what he claims to be the President's blatantly immoral behavior. Mark Luen, in Washington, has that story: Mark."

CHAPTER TWENTY

On the day following the robbery, The Raiders endured yet another loss on the playing field, but there was also encouraging news. Giuseppe asked Devin to bring The Raiders to his office, saying that he and Carlotta wanted to thank them in person, and give them a little token of their gratitude. Devin is excited, and tells them to expect a modest cash reward, or coupons for complimentary drinks or deserts, but warns them that Giuseppe is a stickler for propriety, and will expect them to show up clean-shaven and well-groomed. And this is exactly how they appear, stepping out of Marty's van like self-conscious guests at a formal wedding.

Devin leads them through the back door of the restaurant to Giuseppe's office, and taps on the half-open door.

"Come in. Come in," Giuseppe commands, standing and beckoning them inside.

"Why donna ya troduce everaone to mya Carlotta?" he says, pinching Devin's cheek and gesturing toward Carlotta, who remains seated in a corner, smiling demurely.

"Certainly," Devin agrees.

"Carlotta, these are my good friends: Danny, Marty, Shawn, and Hans. And you know Cruz, of course."

Carlotta smiles and nods to each in turn, as does everyone except Marty, who springs forward to shake her hand, but trips and almost lands in her lap.

"Sita down, sita down," Giuseppe urges, indicating chairs and an over-stuffed couch.

They shuffle, awkwardly, and seat themselves, while Giuseppe returns to the inner-sanctum of his desk, where he sits sizing them up and nodding his head in silent approval. When they are seated, he continues to nod, but more deliberately.

"Giuseppe iza familia, you unastan," he begins.

They don't know whether he is asking a question or making a statement but, inasmuch as he is still nodding, they nod in agreement.

"Anna we look after our own," he continues, "and wadda you boyza did lassa night was a brava thing to do, anna me and my Carlotta we wanna you should have a leetle sometink froma de familia."

He gets up and walks around the desk holding what looks to be banded bundles of hundred dollar bills. He hands the first one to Devin, who stares at it blankly with his mouth open.

"Hold on, boss," he gasps. "This is a helluva lot of dough, and ...."

"Hey, a calma," Giuseppe says, slapping him playfully across the cheek before handing out identical bundles to the others.

"Iza nah much," he continues, "and I ear you boyza trying to collecta da money for a frienda yours, so wadda you do wid da money izza your business, but I tella you what I gonna do. You boyz awanna make a loan fora you fren, we go mya banka, you signa de paper, anna you paya backa de money whena you ready. Jus lika familia, eh? You tella me," he adds.

Once again, they have no idea whether he is making a statement or asking a question, and remain silent. But after Devin has told him about Janie's desperate plight, they all agree to meet at Giuseppe's bank later in the day, to arrange a loan for Joe and Anna.

Minutes later, they emerge from the back door of the restaurant and into the sweltering melting-pot of the valley, blinded by light but renewed by hope.

"Have we got it, or what?" Marty exclaims joyfully.

"It ain't what you've got, Marty," Danny grins, "it's how you use it."